zona

dish
friends, cooking, eating, talking, life.

#4

Into the Mix

S0-AFF-805

The·Post

★ What's the Dish?
Sixth Graders Cook
Up a Business

Honor Student Wins top Prize

Grosset & Dunlap

zone

dish #4

friends, cooking, eating, talking, life.

Into the Mix

By Diane Muldrow

Illustrated by Barbara Pollak

Grosset & Dunlap
New York

For Kelly Muldrow—D.M.

Text copyright © 2002 by Diane Muldrow. Illustrations copyright © 2002 by Barbara Pollak.
All rights reserved. Published by Grosset & Dunlap, a division of Penguin Putnam Books for
Young Readers, 345 Hudson Street, New York, NY, 10014. GROSSET & DUNLAP is a trademark
of Penguin Putnam Inc. Published simultaneously in Canada. Printed in the U.S.A.

Library of Congress Cataloging-in-Publication Data is available.

ISBN 0-448-42829-6   A B C D E F G H I J

chapter 1

To: mooretimes2; qtpie490; BrooklynNatasha
From: happyface
Re: end-of-the-summer bash!

> This summer has been awesome! Can
> u come over to my house on Saturday
> at 1:00 for one last pool party? LMK!
> No need to bring anything—I've
> got it covered!
> Mwa! Peichi ☺ ☺ ☺ ☺

Molly Moore sighed. "I can't believe summer's over," she said as she hit "Reply." She typed:

> GR8! WFM. And Manda 2! Can't W8.
> xxxoo

"W8? I've never seen that one," said Molly's twin, Amanda. "Where did you see that?"

"I just made it up!" Molly told her. "It means 'wait.'"

Amanda giggled. "I figured that out," she said. "Look! Shawn replied." Amanda clicked on Shawn Jordan's e-mail message.

To: happyface; mooretimes2; BrooklynNatasha
From: qtpie490
Re: end-of-the-summer bash!

      I'll be there! Can't wait.
      Shawn

"That just leaves Natasha," said Amanda. "I wonder if she'll be allowed to come."

"I hope so," said Molly. "Let's instant message Shawn. Maybe she's still up." Molly began to type.

To: qtpie490
From: mooretimes2
mooretimes2: Wuzzup qtpie Shawn? We can't WAIT to C u 2morrow and hang out! FINALLY! It's been forever! Your house or ours? BFFL!

A moment later, Shawn Jordan's reply flashed across the screen. Shawn was the twins' best friend. She had just returned from visiting her grandmother and cousins in South Carolina.

qtpie490: How about my place? So you can see G'ma Ruthie . . . who is telling me 2 go 2 bed right now! TTUL! Mwa! <3   <3   <3

"Well, I don't feel like going to bed now," Amanda said.

"I can't sleep. I'm too excited about school starting."

"*Excited?*" Molly said. "I'm *nervous!*"

"I'll bet our new school has a website. Let's check it out," Amanda said.

"*Aaagh!*" Molly suddenly cried out.

"Come on, Molls, school won't be that bad—uh, oh, hi Dad," Amanda said with a giggle. "So *that's* what scared you!"

"Hi, girls! What are you doing down here so late?" asked Mr. Moore. "I thought you were in bed."

"Oh, we couldn't sleep," said Molly. "What are *you* doing down here, Dad? Did you come downstairs for some cookies?"

"Cookies?" asked Dad innocently. "Oh, no. Just checking to make sure the doors are locked, that sort of thing." He yawned. "You know, as long as I'm down here, I think I'll get a nice, cold glass of water from the pitcher in the fridge."

The twins giggled. The family knew Dad loved his late-night snacks, even though he tried to hide them.

"Here it is!" said Amanda. She'd found the website for Windsor Middle School. They looked at the photos of the teachers and classes and sports teams, and read all about what a wonderful place Windsor was supposed to be.

"It seems okay," said Molly, "for a moldy old school."

"I think it looks great!" exclaimed Amanda.

The next morning, the girls couldn't wait to see Shawn. Right after breakfast, they headed straight over to her apartment.

"How *are* you guys?" Shawn said as she opened the door. She hugged the twins.

"We missed you so much!" Molly said. She stepped back and looked at Shawn. "Wow!" she exclaimed. "You've grown, like, another foot!"

"You look like a model!" added Amanda. "And I love your outfit!" Shawn was wearing white shorts and a pink peasant top, which looked great against her coffee-colored skin.

Shawn laughed, embarrassed. "Thanks," she said. "You both look good, too! So, what have you guys been up to?"

"We just got back from Poppy's last night," said Molly. Poppy was the twins' grandfather, who had a big house on the New Jersey shore. The twins and their seven-year-old brother, Matthew, had been at the beach with Poppy and their parents every day for the last week, collecting shells, bodysurfing, and hanging out on the boardwalk.

"Where's Grandma Ruthie?" asked Amanda.

Shawn's Grandma Ruthie was staying with Shawn while her dad was away on a business trip in Australia. Shawn's mom had died a few years ago, so when her dad had to go away, Grandma Ruthie came to stay. Shawn loved her grandma, but she still really missed her mom a lot.

"She's out on the terrace," said Shawn, leading the girls outside.

"Hi, Grandma Ruthie!" called the twins.

Grandma Ruthie was relaxing on the chaise longue. She looked up from her newspaper. Her face was plump and friendly. She had wavy gray hair and big blue glasses.

"Look who's here!" said Grandma Ruthie. "Hello, girls! Now, wait, wait, tell me who's who. I'm never gonna be able to tell you two apart."

Before the twins could say anything, Shawn said, "Oh, that's easy, Grandma. Molly almost always wears a pony-tail, and Amanda dresses up more than Molly does."

The twins looked at each other and giggled. It was true. Amanda was wearing a denim halter, white capris, glittery plastic flip-flops, and lip gloss. Molly's hair was up in a high pony. She was wearing cargo shorts, a T-shirt, and boys' blue canvas sneakers.

"Want to cook something?" Shawn asked after the girls went inside. "I've really missed cooking with you."

"Sure," said Molly.

"I'm in the mood for some adventure," Shawn said. "Let's make whatever I open our cookbook to."

"Try to open it on a dessert!" Amanda pleaded.

Shawn pulled a cookbook off the shelf and set it on the table. Closing her eyes, she slid a finger under a page and flipped open the book.

"Shawn, what are you doing?" said Grandma Ruthie with a laugh. She had come inside to refill her empty iced-tea glass.

"I'm trying to find a new recipe," Shawn replied.

"Is that how you decide what you feed your poor clients?" She shook her head again, and the girls laughed.

The clients that Grandma Ruthie was talking about were all the people that the girls had cooked for over the summer. The friends had their own little cooking business, called Dish!

"Now, shoo," said Grandma Ruthie as she filled her iced-tea glass. "I want you girls out of this kitchen. Go outside. It's a beautiful day!"

"You're right, Grandma Ruthie," said Shawn with a laugh. "We don't want to be stuck inside the kitchen today—especially with the oven on!"

"I thought we were going to get school supplies anyway," said Amanda. "Let's go!"

"Do you want to see if Peichi and Natasha can meet us?" asked Molly.

"Natasha?" asked Shawn. "Well, okay. I'll call Peichi if you call Natasha."

"Okay," said Molly. Picking up the phone, she said to Shawn, "I know things were weird with Natasha before you left. But a lot's happened since you went away. Things are better now."

"I know," said Shawn, nodding. She smiled. "That's cool. But I'll have to get used to the fact that she's not mean anymore!"

Natasha used to be the girls' arch enemy—spreading mean rumors about them around school. But over the summer, they had discovered another side to Natasha— a nicer side. Now she was part of their group.

After a few quick phone calls, Molly and Shawn arranged for Peichi and Natasha to meet them at "Turtle Bench" in Prospect Park. They'd named it Turtle Bench because it faced the lake, near the home of many turtles.

"Hi, Shawn!" called Peichi Cheng as she bounded toward the bench with her shiny black hair swinging behind her. "Wow, you look awesome! How was your trip? When did you get back? Are you glad to be home?"

Shawn laughed as she hugged Peichi. *This girl can talk!* Shawn thought to herself. "I can see you haven't changed, Peichi," Shawn said with a smile. "South Carolina was great! But I'm glad to be home, too. I've missed all you guys. And I've missed New York."

Natasha Ross soon showed up. She was wearing a tie-dyed tank top with a cute denim skirt. "Hi, Shawn," she said softly. "Welcome back."

"Hi, Natasha, how's your summer been?" asked Shawn.

"Good." Natasha answered.

"Mine too." Shawn smiled. She cleared her throat. She really didn't know what to say after that. After all, she hadn't spent much time with the "nice" Natasha.

"Well—it's t-i-i-i-ime to go shop-ping!" said Amanda in a TV announcer's voice. "Let's go to the drug store. Molly and I need notebooks and pens and all that stuff."

So did everyone else.

"What's everyone wearing on the first day of school?" asked Amanda as the friends walked down the hill to Park Terrace, the girls' Brooklyn neighborhood. "I can't decide, and it's driving me crazy!"

"I'm wearing my pink skirt and my striped peasant top," said Peichi. "I mean, it's still summer. We can't wear fall clothes yet. But I haven't figured out how to wear my hair! What do you guys think? Up or down?"

"Up," said Molly and Natasha.

"Down," said Amanda and Shawn.

Peichi giggled. "You guys are no help!"

"I don't know what to wear either," said Molly. "I wish our school just had uniforms."

Amanda rolled her eyes. "*Uniforms?* Why?"

"'Cause it would be so much easier," replied Molly. "Just think—you'd never have to wonder what to wear! And you'd never have to put anything together and worry whether it matches or not!"

"Molly, you're probably the only kid who ever *wanted* to wear a uniform," Amanda said.

"Actually," Peichi broke in, "Some kids like uniforms. St. Theresa's School has cute uniforms. *I'd* wear them."

"Don't worry, Molls," Amanda went on. "I'll tell you what to wear on the first day of school—and every day after that."

"Good," said Molly. "That's fine with me." She smiled at her sister.

"Speaking of clothes, do you want to go look in Lulu's Closet? Remember, we have those gift certificates from Poppy," Amanda said.

"I *love* that store!" cried Peichi. "Come on, let's go!"

"But what about our school supplies?" Molly asked.

"That can wait!" Amanda told her. "Clothes shopping is so much more fun."

"If you say so," Molly said. "I guess we can get them later." She followed the rest of the girls to Lulu's.

The girls loved the funky clothes made by Lulu, a young Brooklyn fashion designer whose hair color changed every week. She always used unique buttons and unusual fabrics. Her clothes weren't like the same old things from the mall that everybody wore.

"*Oooh*, this is so great!" cried Peichi, pulling a fake fur jacket off the rack. "A leopard-print coat with a matching belt! Amanda, try this on."

"I love it," said Amanda, "but my mom wants us to get something we'll really wear a lot. Here—look at this corduroy skirt. I love the purple color. Natasha, this would look good on you."

After a while, Molly got bored. "Is anybody hungry?" she asked.

"I am!" cried Peichi. "Let's get lunch at Harry's."

"Okay," said everyone, and they headed to their favorite hangout.

The twins and Shawn had discovered Harry's when it first opened several months earlier. Writers, artists, and students were always sitting around the small marble tables, sipping tea or coffee out of colorful, mismatched china cups. Music from all over the world played on the restaurant's stereo. The girls liked Harry's because it was so cool. They felt older than eleven whenever they sat and ate veggie wraps and drank iced tea.

It had been only recently that the girls had been allowed to go to a place like Harry's without their parents. Now, as long as they were in a group of two or more, they were able to walk to the cool toy stores, pizzerias, bookstores, and movie theaters that were all within a few tree-lined blocks of their homes.

There was so much to do and see in Park Terrace. Most

of the girls lived within a few blocks of Prospect Park. The park had a big lake with pedal boats, a new zoo, an old carousel, beautiful meadows, and a bandshell. The girls' parents often took them there to see free concerts, dance performances, and plays. There was also an ice-skating rink and a nature center.

Outside the park was the Brooklyn Library, a huge art museum, and the botanic gardens. Just a subway ride away, under the East River, was the island of Manhattan—otherwise known as The Big Apple. New York City.

"Hey, look who it is!" exclaimed Molly, as two boys sitting on a bench outside of Harry's waved at them. "Hi, Connor. Hi, Omar. What are *you* doing here? This is *our* hangout."

All the girls knew Connor Kelly and Omar Kazdan from the cooking course they'd taken at Park Terrace Cookware over the summer. Omar and Connor had been the class clowns. Freckle-faced Connor and dark-eyed Omar were always joking around with each other.

"We don't hang out at this sissy place," said Connor. "We're just holding up the wall. It's shady here."

"Well, they're gonna come out here and tell you that you have to buy something," Molly teased him.

Omar slapped his forehead. "I just remembered! The pizza place just reopened. Let's go and get some slices."

"Wanna come?" Connor asked the girls.

A slice of pizza and a cold soda sounded good to everyone. They all headed over to Pizza Roma.

"Ladies first!" cracked Connor when the friends reached the counter. "That means you, Omar!"

"Very funny, *not!*" said Omar. "Go ahead, Molly."

"A plain slice, not too hot," Molly told the man at the counter.

"Plain slice! Not too hot!" he bellowed to the bored-looking teenager in charge of cutting and heating the pizza. The man turned to Molly and asked, "Something-to-dreenk?"

"Um, a root beer, please," said Molly.

"Small-medium-large?" asked the counterman impatiently.

"Oh, a—medium." Molly turned to Connor and Omar. "Are you guys going to Windsor?" she asked them.

"Two pepperoni! One plain!" bellowed the counterman as the other girls placed their orders. "Something-to-dreenk?"

"I'm going to Windsor," replied Connor over the pizza man's shouts. He looked sadly at Omar. "Poor Omar's heading off to reform school."

"Am not!" said Omar, slapping Connor playfully on

the head. "Don't listen to him. I'm going to Windsor, too. Big deal. We'll be at the bottom of the food chain. The little guys. The ones the seventh- and eighth-graders will pick on."

"Yeah," said Connor, "but next year it'll be *our* turn to pick on kids! I'll make some poor sixth-grader carry my backpack."

Everyone chuckled. They knew Connor didn't have a mean bone in his body.

The group sat down at a large booth.

"I wonder when we'll get our schedules," said Peichi.

"I hope I don't get Mr. Carlson for Science," Omar told the friends. "You know what my big brother told me? That he makes you dissect a frog—on the first day of school!"

Natasha and Amanda nearly choked on their slices.

"Dissect? You mean, like, cut it open?" asked Connor, going pale under his freckles.

"No way," said Molly.

"I don't believe it either," said Shawn, coolly sipping her soda. "You don't dissect a frog until high school."

"I hope not!" cried Peichi. "Ugh!"

"What about Miss Spontak?" asked Molly. "I hear she's the hardest math teacher in the whole school. She gives pop quizzes every day at the beginning of class!"

"Not *every* day," protested Natasha, frowning. "Nobody does *that.*"

"I've heard that about her, too," Shawn told Natasha.

"And then there's Mr. Snell!" said Connor. "They say he wears the same shirt and pants the *whole week!*"

"Get outta here!" protested Shawn.

"It's true!" said Omar. "You've never heard of Snell the Smell?"

The girls put down their slices of pizza and groaned.

Molly just sat there as her friends joked around about all the nasty teachers they might get. All this talk about middle school had made her lose her appetite. Molly loved school last year. But she was sure that middle school would be awful. New school. New kids. New teachers. Molly wished September would never come. With a sigh, she drank some soda.

"Hey, there's Justin and Ian," said Shawn, waving at two boys walking past the pizzeria window.

Amanda began to blush.

Don't say anything, don't say anything, Amanda's eyes warned the girls. Amanda would have died if Connor and Omar found out that she had a crush on Justin.

The two brothers stopped and peered in the window, then waved. They turned around to come in.

"I've seen them around," said Connor.

"They're new," Amanda told him. "The McElroys. They're our neighbors."

"Hi,'" said Justin and Ian.

"Hi, Justin. Hi, Ian," the girls answered.

"This is Connor, and this is Omar," said Amanda. "This is Justin, and this is Ian."

"How ya doin'," said Justin and Ian. Both boys had reddish-brown hair and brown eyes, but Ian had dyed the front of his hair blond.

"What's up, man," said Connor. Omar nodded.

"We just got our schedules in the mail," said Justin. "For school."

"Really?" the girls said. *"Ohmygosh!"*

"Who did you get?" asked Amanda.

Justin looked at her blankly. "For which class?" he asked.

Amanda immediately felt stupid. "Um, for—math," she said, recovering.

Justin had to think. "Um, Pontok? Spontok? Something like that?"

Everyone at the table groaned. "Spontak!" they cried.

"What? Is that bad?" asked Justin, looking flustered.

"Not if you like pop quizzes," Connor told him. "Every day. Good luck, man."

"I'm not worried about it," said Justin, shrugging. "I'm good at math. Well, see you guys later."

"See ya," said Ian.

"Byeeee!" cried Peichi.

"Byeeee!" cried Omar in a high voice, imitating Peichi. Everyone cracked up.

Amanda sipped the last of her orange soda and put down the paper cup. "Are you ready to go?" she asked the other girls. "I'm dying to see if we got our schedules."

"I'm not," said Molly.

"Why not?" Connor asked her.

"Because once I get my schedule, that's it! Summer's over!" replied Molly.

"Don't worry, Molly! Summer's not over yet— we still have my pool party," said Peichi.

"You mean we could have been swimming at your house all summer after cooking class?" joked Connor.

"Sorry, the party's for girls only!" said Peichi with a giggle. "No boys allowed."

"Well," said Omar, getting up, "See ya."

"See ya," said the girls. The group went outside, and Connor and Omar walked away.

"Come over to our house as soon as you get your schedules," Amanda told Shawn, Natasha, and Peichi.

"Good luck!" said Peichi. "I hope no one gets Snell the Smell!"

"Snell the Smell!" groaned the girls. They walked for a few blocks together, then waved as the twins turned up Taft Street, their pretty tree-lined block.

When the twins got home, their mom was already back from work. Her dark eyes twinkled as she said, "You got something in the mail today!" She handed them each a packet.

16

"*Yes!* It's our schedules!" said Amanda. She tore the envelope open and quickly looked down the list.

"Spontak," whined Molly. "I got Spontak. I can't believe it."

"What's Spontak?" asked Mom. "It sounds like a disease."

"Spontak is a person. Miss Spontak the math teacher. She's terrible!" said Amanda. "She gives pop quizzes every day!"

"Now, hang on, maybe she's not so bad," said Mom. "Maybe she's a great teacher!"

"At least you'll be in Justin's class," said Amanda enviously.

Molly shrugged. "Who cares? I'm not the one who likes him, remember?"

"Molly," said Mom in her "warning" voice. "Don't talk to your sister like that."

"I've never heard of any of my teachers," said Amanda. "So maybe that's a good thing!"

"Let's see your schedule," said Molly, suddenly worried. She and Amanda laid their schedules next to each other on the kitchen counter. Their eyes flitted back and forth, from Molly's to Amanda's.

"We don't have any classes together!" exclaimed Molly.

c h a p t e r 2

"That can't be," said Amanda, still looking. But it was true. The twins didn't have a single class together.

"Oh, no!" cried Amanda.

The twins looked at each other. They were having "the twin thing." They were both thinking that, until now, they'd never been apart during the school day.

"That's gonna be so weird," groaned Amanda.

"Uh-huh," said Molly sadly.

Within minutes, Peichi, Natasha, and Shawn had all shown up at the Moore's. Each girl had her schedule.

"Let's go out to the garden," said Molly, leading the way through the kitchen.

The girls breathed in the scent of the honeysuckle that grew along the fence. "*Mmm*, that smells awesome!" everyone cried.

"Can you believe that Amanda and I don't have any classes together?" asked Molly. "Except homeroom?"

"No way!" cried Shawn. "That's terrible. You guys are *twins*. That should be, like, illegal."

"Okay," said Amanda, "let's check these out." She laid everyone's schedules on the picnic table where

18

the Moores ate dinner during the summer. The friends hovered over them together. For a moment, all was quiet as they looked everything over.

"Oh!" cried Peichi. "Amanda, you're in my English class. Great!"

"So am I!" said Shawn. "And it looks like Natasha and I are in math together. The teacher is Smith."

"Is anyone in social studies during fourth period?" asked Molly. "The teacher is Epstein."

"No," said all the girls, squinting at their schedules.

Molly tried again. "Gym, third period?"

"No."

"Nope."

"Uh-uh."

"Look, Peichi, you and I are in gym together," said Natasha. "And computer training first period."

"Great!" said Peichi. "I like my schedule! We have gym at the end of the day—that's perfect!"

"Wait a minute!" said Molly, a lump growing in her throat. The girls stopped talking and laughing and looked at her.

"Aren't *any* of you in *any* of my classes?" she asked.

"Let's see," said Shawn, moving Molly's schedule to the center of the table. "I have social studies the same time you do, but with Reese, not Epstein..."

Natasha and Peichi studied Molly's schedule, then shook their heads.

"I can't believe it, Molly," said Peichi. "You're not with us at all! That's terrible! I feel so bad!"

Molly didn't say anything. She looked down, and her lower lip trembled.

"Gee, Molls, that stinks," said Amanda. "At least we all have lunch together. You can sit smack in the middle of all of us every day! Okay?"

Saturday came, the day of Peichi's pool party. The Moores were having their traditional Saturday morning pancake breakfast in their large, colorful kitchen. The kitchen, with its pale-yellow walls bordered with blue and green tiles, and cheerful rugs that were shaped like apples and pears, was the twins' favorite room in the house. The girls usually cooked for their clients in the Moores' kitchen because it was so large.

Amanda sighed. "I'm full. That was so good, Dad." Dad didn't cook often, but he did make awesome pancakes.

"Thanks," said Dad. He looked at Molly's plate. "You didn't eat much, Molly," he pointed out. "Are you feeling okay?"

"Uh-huh," Molly said with a nod. But the truth was that her stomach felt tight every time she thought about school starting on Monday.

Which was all the time.

"Are you girls supposed to bring something to Peichi's party?" asked Mom, as she poured some more coffee.

"No," said Amanda. "She said she had it covered."

"That's sweet, but I still think you should bring something. How about making Dad's favorite— seven layer dip? You can bring a big bag of tortilla chips along, too," Mom suggested.

"Yum!" cried Matthew. "Can I help?"

"Help eat it, that's what you really mean," cracked Amanda.

"No, I want to help make it," insisted Matthew.

"*Mrow*," said Kitty, Matthew's fat tiger cat. Kitty was sitting on the extra chair at the kitchen table, next to Matthew. She liked being in the middle of everything the family did.

"Okay, Kitty, Matthew can help," said Amanda. Kitty adored Matthew, even when he made her wear ball caps or sunglasses, or held her in positions that didn't look too comfortable.

An hour later, everyone was back in the kitchen with Mom (except for Dad, who was outside taking a nap under the sports section of *The New York Times*). Molly turned on the radio.

"Okay. The first thing we need to do is make some guacamole for the dip. Amanda, you can peel the skins off these avocados for the guacamole...Molls, you can chop the tomatoes. I'll do the cilantro."

"Hey, what about me?" Matthew asked, his hands on his hips.

"Let's see," Mom said. "Why don't you get started on layering the dip. That's an important job!"

Matthew smiled.

Mom opened a can of refried beans and handed it to Matthew with a glass pie plate. "Spread these all over the bottom of this plate."

"Eeew! Beans!" Matthew made a face. "Bean, beans, are good for your heart. The more you eat, the more you..."

"Very funny," Amanda said, rolling her eyes.

"Like we haven't heard that one before," Molly added.

After Amanda finished peeling the avocados, she put them in a bowl and mashed them with a fork. Then the tomatoes and cilantro were mixed into the avocados.

"I think we should add some garlic to the guacamole," Mom said, placing a garlic clove in a press.

"Now what?" asked Matthew.

"On top of the beans, we'll spread some sour cream," Mom told them. "Then some guacamole, and then some cheese."

"What kind?" Molly asked.

"How about a mixture," Amanda suggested. "Like jack and cheddar."

After the cheese was layered on, they added the

tomatoes, green onions, and finally some black olives.

"It looks pretty," said Amanda. "Everyone's gonna love this!"

Later, as the girls swam in the Cheng's pool, Peichi brought out her parents' video camera.

"Okay, Chef Girls," she announced. "Everyone has to tell me their favorite thing that happened this summer."

Looking through the viewfinder, she said, "I'm here at my pool, interviewing the Chef Girls about this amazingly fantastic summer. Amanda Moore, please tell us your favorite thing about it."

Amanda waved at the camera. "Hi," she said. "Well, I guess it was when—"

Molly stuck her head into view. "When she got to give the food we cooked to Justin McElroy!" She made kissing sounds and funny faces at the camera, then ran and jumped into the pool with a big splash.

"It was not!" cried Amanda, blushing. "That's a do-over, Peichi."

Molly was talking about the first time the girls cooked for someone else. The twins' new neighbors, the McElroys, had a small electrical fire in their kitchen, and their kitchen had been off-limits while the fire damage was getting repaired. It made the girls feel good to help out Justin and his family, and the McElroys had been delighted when the girls showed up with boxes of food they'd made with Mrs. Moore's help.

The girls now made money with Dish, their brand-new cooking business, but they all agreed that they would still cook for free when someone in their neighborhood needed help.

"Go ahead, Amanda," said Peichi.

"Um, okay," said Amanda, smoothing down her wet hair as she talked into the camera. "My favorite thing about this summer was...taking our cooking class and getting to eat all the yummy food afterward! And I love the cookbook we're making." The girls wrote down every recipe they learned in a cool blank book that they illustrated with Shawn's glitter pens and watercolors.

"Great!" said Peichi. "You're next, Natasha."

Natasha was sitting at the table under the umbrella. "This dip is awesome!" she said. Natasha wiped her mouth with a paper napkin. "I don't want to be on film," she said, covering her face with her hands.

"Come on, don't be shy!" said Peichi.

Natasha tucked her blond hair behind her ears, grinned at the camera, and said, "The best thing about this summer? Getting to know you guys better, and becoming one of the Chef Girls!" She blushed and waved the camera away.

"You're on, Molly," said Peichi, pointing the camera at

Molly, who was sitting on the edge of the pool eating potato chips.

"Well, Amanda and I thought we were going to have a horrible, boring summer," Molly began, as she looked into the camera. "Amanda and I were so sick of eating the take-out food our busy parents kept bringing home, that one boring, *boring* day, we found a recipe for chicken piccata on the Internet and made it for our family. And it was so good, even our finicky brother ate it. And we'd never even cooked before! And then right after that, Shawn *finally* came back from vacation—for a while, anyway—and then right after *that*, we heard about the cooking class, and we got to know *you* better in class, Peichi, and then Natasha, too—and now we actually have our own cooking business and we make money! And—"

"Okay, cut!" said Peichi. "That's way more than one thing!"

Molly was out of breath. "I can't choose," she said with a laugh.

Shawn came up for air.

"Shawn, your turn!" called Peichi.

Shawn got out of the pool and draped a towel over herself in an elegant way. "How do I look?" she joked.

"Like a drowned rat," replied Peichi. "Just kidding! Go ahead."

"Hi," said Shawn to the camera. "Let me see...my visits down South with Grandma Ruthie and my cousins

Sonia and Jamal was amazing. We rode horses, we went to the beach, Sonia showed me all her cheerleading moves, and Grandma Ruthie made me laugh all the time. And in New York, there was cooking class, and starting Dish, and cooking for all kinds of people, and making money doing it. And your pool parties. It's all been fun!"

"Okay, it's my turn!" announced Peichi. "Molly, can you hold the camera? Thanks...The best part of *my* summer. Well, getting a pool was amazing! And my redecorated room is so great. And Dish is awesome. But the best thing has been becoming friends with everybody here! Because we always have a blast. This year together in school is gonna be *great!* Watch out, Windsor Middle School!"

"*Woo-hoo!*" yelled all the girls.

Even Molly tried to look excited.

On Monday morning, the first day of school, the alarm seemed extra loud.

Amanda sat straight up in bed before she turned off the alarm. She looked over at Molly, who was on her side, curled up in a ball. "Molls," said Amanda. "Get up."

But Molly was already awake. She'd been awake practically the whole night.

"Okay." Molly sighed and rolled over to see Amanda. *Now* she felt tired. "Are you nervous, Manda?"

"No!" said Amanda. "I'm psyched! It's going to be fun to meet all kinds of new people! I know exactly what I'm going to wear, and it's all laid out, and my hair's gonna look so cute 'cause I'm going to wear my new barrettes, and I can't wait to show off my new backpack! I already put a packet of tissues in it—"

She's nervous all right, Molly thought to herself. *What a motormouth.*

Just then, the door opened. It was Mom, still in her funny pj's with pictures of bacon and eggs on them. "Happy first day of middle school!" she said. "Are you girls up?"

"Hi, Mom!" cried Amanda, jumping out of bed.

27

"Hi, Mom," mumbled Molly.

"What are you wearing today, Molly?" asked Mom.

"Oh, she's wearing the stretch denim capris and the green shirt with the collar," Amanda answered for her. "And my new sneakers. Don't worry, I'm on it." She walked over and pulled her sister out of bed.

"Good," said Mom. "There's no time for a wardrobe panic. Breakfast in ten minutes." She closed the door and went to wake Matthew.

No one said much at breakfast, except for Dad, who kept cracking corny jokes. Mom never said much in the mornings, but she seemed to be smiling extra sweetly today, as if to say, *Everything's going to be okay!*

Molly drank all her grape juice, but it was hard to finish her oatmeal. She went up ahead of Amanda to brush her teeth.

Staring at herself in the mirror, she thought to herself, *Well, today's the day. It's gonna be great! I'm gonna make new friends...and it's not like I'm really losing my old friends anyway. But maybe I'll be invisible...oh, I want to be at the beach right now with Poppy...*

Just then, Amanda walked in. "What are you doing in here? You ready? We've got to go!" She picked up her toothbrush. "We have to meet Shawn in five minutes. Don't forget your schedule! And your lip balm!"

"Okay," said Molly. The beach was forgotten. She sighed and went to get her backpack and to

28

check for the millionth time if her schedule was inside.

On the walk to school, the twins picked up Shawn. Natasha and Peichi said they would meet them at the school gate.

Shawn looked amazing, as usual. She wore a cute sleeveless denim dress, belted. And she had a new bag made out of blue denim slung across her body. It was like a bicycle messenger bag. *The perfect outfit for the first day of school,* thought Amanda enviously. Amanda suddenly felt that her aqua top was all wrong. It was too bright. It made her stand out too much.

Shawn was completely calm. "Hi, guys," she said. Nothing fazed her! *How can that be?* wondered Molly.

"Well, here we go!" said Amanda.

After the girls met up with Natasha and Peichi they all walked through the double doors together, joking and laughing loudly to hide their nervousness. Sunlight streamed through the high windows. WELCOME STUDENTS, said one huge sign. GO WINDSOR WARRIORS! said another. The main hall was full of shrieks, shouts, and laughter.

The halls seemed to go on forever, and they were covered in gleaming blue tiles that rippled through the beige walls.

"Wow!" cried Molly. "Some of these kids look huge, like they're in high school! I feel like a shrimp!"

A bell rang so loudly that the girls jumped.

"We have to get to homeroom!" said Peichi. *"Ohmygosh!* Byeee! I have to go that way! See you at lunch or maybe before, I can't remember! Have fun!"

All the girls said good-bye and shuffled along with the crowd to find their homerooms. Molly and Amanda walked into room 12B, found two seats next to each other, and looked around for people they knew from Jefferson Elementary. Some kids looked bored, some looked scared, and some were chatting with people they knew.

Just then, a tan, lanky man walked in. He wore khakis and a pale-blue button-down shirt. His eyes were a steely blue. His thick brown hair was brushed straight back and he had a hooked nose. *He looks like a bird,* thought Molly, *like an eagle. Some people just look like animals...*

"I'm Mr. Flint," the man told the class. "This is home-room. Sixth grade. If you're not in sixth grade, this may not be the class for you."

There was silence.

"That's a joke, people." Mr. Flint's face cracked into a tight smile. Everyone laughed weakly.

"Three minutes," said Mr. Flint. He paused and his eagle eyes flickered around the room. "You have three minutes to change classes. It's not much time. Don't waste time."

Another long pause.

Both Molly and Amanda could hear their hearts beating in their ears.

"Lockouts," said Mr. Flint. "What are lockouts? I'll tell you. A lockout comes without warning. One day you're supposed to be in your classroom. You're almost there. Almost. But you're still talking to your friends. Or you're trying to shut your locker. You hear an announcement over the loudspeaker. It says: 'This is a lockout. Any student not in his or her seat has detention for tardiness and must report to the Main Office.'" Mr. Flint paused and looked around the room.

"The Main Office," he went on. "Trust me. You don't want to report there. Ever."

A girl giggled nervously until Mr. Flint shot her a look.

"Use your three minutes, people. Take control of your destiny. Don't be a victim of a lockout." Mr. Flint looked down at the floor, as if to give the students time to think. Then he quickly raised his head and reached for a notebook. His sharp eyes slowly moved up and down the rows.

"It's time for attendance," he said. "Mathers. John."

A boy cleared his throat. "Um, here," he said.

Mr. Flint stared straight ahead. "Where?"

The boy raised his hand. "Over here, sir."

Mr. Flint slowly turned his head to his right to look at John, who'd turned beet red.

"Matthews. Benjamin."

Benjamin knew to raise his hand and say, "Here."

Oh, boy, thought Amanda.

Gimme a break, thought Molly.

After homeroom, Molly and Amanda had to split up.

"See you at lunch, Molls," said Amanda. "Remember, we're all meeting up in front of the cafeteria."

"Okay, bye," said Molly. She waved to her sister.

For all the girls, the rest of the morning was a blur of loud bells, crowds of students rushing in a panic to find their next class, scurrying up and down steps. Meeting one new teacher after the next.

And then there was gym.

Changing clothes in front of everyone else. Trying not to look at anyone else as they changed into the horrifying gymsuit. No one looked good in it, not even Shawn. Striped on top, solid below the elasticized waist, it was the school colors of red and white.

Finally, it was time for lunch.

Molly was the last one there. She found the others pointing to a bulletin board studded with announcements.

"How's Spontak?" Amanda asked Molly. "Is Justin in your class?"

"How about those gym suits?" joked Shawn. "Well, Molly, you got your uniform!" Everyone laughed.

"Justin's in my class," reported Molly. "Actually, Miss

Spontak seems okay. Some kid actually asked her if it's true that she gives a pop quiz every day!"

"What did she say?"

"She laughed and said that's an urban legend."

"What's an urban legend?" asked Peichi.

"I guess it's, like, a really weird story that gets passed around," replied Molly with a shrug. "Anyway, she does give a quiz once a week. Every Friday, to make sure we learned everything from the week. That's not so bad."

"Omar's in two of my classes," reported Shawn. "He's really quiet without Connor! Hey, look! Cheerleading tryouts are this Friday!" She pointed up at the announcement. "*Yessss!* I'm there. I've been practicing all summer for this."

"I'm gonna try out, too," said Amanda. "I'm ready."

"What?" said Molly. "You've never mentioned cheerleading."

"Oh, Molly, I have so," said Amanda impatiently.

"Sixth-graders never make it," muttered Molly.

"I don't know what to go out for," said Peichi. "I'm learning Chinese now, too. I don't know if I have time for anything else."

"I know what you mean," Natasha told Peichi. "I have Hebrew school in the afternoons. But I really want to work on <u>The Post</u>, the school paper. 'Cause I want to be a reporter when I grow up."

"I thought you wanted to be a lawyer," said Molly.

"No, I changed my mind."

Molly looked at all the announcements. *"Check' It Out! Chess Club starts September 12...Windsor Volunteers Make a Difference in Brooklyn—join us next Tuesday!... Intramurals for Everyone! Field Hockey, Soccer, Come on Out!"*

But nothing sounded very exciting to her.

"C'mon, let's go in," suggested Shawn. "I'm starved."

"I hope the food isn't too bad!" exclaimed Peichi. "But I have granola bars for everyone just in case!"

"I didn't know you were going out for cheerleading," Molly told Amanda after dinner, as they sat in their large room flipping through their new textbooks.

"You didn't? Oh, yeah, Shawn and I are gonna have so much fun. If we make it. We'll get to wear our cheerleading uniforms to school on game days. The whole school will know who we are. Then we won't just be shrimpy little sixth-graders, Molls. We'll be sixth-grade *cheerleaders.* That'll make such a difference. It's *important* to try to be popular now, at the very beginning. You know? Everything will be so much easier!"

"Oh," said Molly. She wasn't so sure.

Amanda began writing some notes in her notebook, but then she looked up at Molly. "You really should go out for *some* activity, Molls. Don't you want to meet new people? Don't you want to be popular?"

Molly snorted. "Of course I do!" she said. "I know I'll make friends. I always do. Easier than you do...sorry. I shouldn't have said that."

Amanda nodded. "You're right, you do," she stated matter-of-factly.

"Anyway," Molly went on, "all I care about is that I have good friends that I have fun with. I don't care if I'm *popular* or not. That doesn't matter to me. And it shouldn't matter to you."

Amanda shut her social studies textbook and looked at her sister. "Good point," she admitted. "You're right about that. But, Molly, aren't you excited at *all* about middle school?"

"Sure," squeaked Molly. Her voice always squeaked when she was faking enthusiasm. She opened her math textbook. "But this summer was great. It was the best summer ever. Aren't you sad that it's over?"

"Well, yeah, but there's always next summer," said Amanda with a shrug.

Next summer, thought Molly, *that's not until forever.*

4

"GO, GO, GO! GO MIGHTY WARRIORS! GO, GO, GO! GO MIGHTY WARRIORS!" shouted the cheerleader hopefuls.

Amanda was breathing hard, and the tryouts weren't even halfway over. She was tired. They'd jogged, stretched, and done splits and dozens of cartwheels in front of Coach Carson, the athletic gym teacher. Now the girls were learning cheers and the moves that went with them.

Shawn stood right in front, while Amanda hid out toward the back. She realized that a lot of the other girls were much better at this stuff than she was.

Next to Shawn was a tall girl with olive skin and long blond hair. She looked older, but Amanda overheard her tell the coach in a shrill, sharp voice that she was in sixth grade. Amanda watched her talking and joking with Shawn. During a break, when Amanda went up to Shawn, the girl interrupted her—and ignored her, too. She talked to Shawn as if Amanda wasn't even there.

"This is my friend, Amanda," Shawn told the girl. "Amanda, this is Angie."

"Hi," said Amanda.

Angie barely nodded, barely looked at Amanda, then she began talking to Shawn again.

Ugh, thought Amanda. *What's with this girl?*

Later, after each girl had cheered, clapped, and jumped her heart out, Coach Carson said, "Thanks, everyone. We'll post the list tomorrow."

Amanda was relieved when the whole thing was over. "Come on, let's change," she told Shawn. "I'm starved."

"See ya, Shawn!" called Angie as the girls walked out of the locker room. She didn't say good-bye to Amanda.

"How was it?" Molly asked Amanda when she got home. "How'd ya do?"

"Pretty good!" said Amanda. "I mean, I wasn't the best person there. But I was okay. One thing's for sure—I'm gonna be sore tomorrow!"

That night, as Amanda tried to sleep, she couldn't get the cheers out of her mind. She finally dozed off, imagining herself in a cheerleading outfit...THAT'S ALL RIGHT! THAT'S OKAY! WE'RE GONNA BEAT 'EM ANYWAY!

When Amanda woke up the next morning, she was nervous.

As she washed her face, she kept thinking, *What if I don't make it? Everything's gonna be ruined.* But then she'd picture herself and Shawn in front of a crowd in their cute uniforms, cheering their hearts out, and she thought, *Nothing could be cooler than that. We've got to make it!*

"Is something the matter, Manda?" asked Dad at breakfast. "You look like you don't feel well."

"I feel *fine*, Dad," said Amanda, rolling her eyes. "Don't you remember what *day* it is?"

Dad looked hurt.

"Sorry, Dad," said Amanda, looking down at her toast. When she looked up, her family was looking at her blankly. Even Molly.

"Today's the day we find out about cheerleading," Amanda reminded everyone. She used her most patient voice, but she was thinking, *Duh! Hello! Like, what else is there right now?*

"Oh, right," said everyone.

Forty-five minutes later, as the twins and Shawn walked into the school, it seemed to Amanda that the crowd seemed more hyper than usual. There was a buzz that filled the halls. Everyone seemed to be talking about the same thing: who made cheerleading...*Or is it just my imagination?* wondered Amanda, as she walked through the crowd.

There it was up ahead, the bulletin board with the list. A dozen girls were reading it. Some were shrieking happily when they spotted their names. But most were stone-faced as their eyes scanned the lists one more time before they walked away. Some seventh- and eighth-grade girls and guys were reading the list out of curiosity, pointing to the names of the girls they knew.

"Here goes, Shawn," said Amanda, grabbing Shawn's hand. For some reason, her ears ached.

"Your hands are freezing!" exclaimed Shawn. She giggled. Of course, Shawn wasn't nervous at all. She seemed to already know that she'd made it.

And she had.

"All *right!*" cried Shawn. "There I am!" She pointed to her name at the top of the second column. "*Ohmygosh!* I made it!"

"That's great, Shawn!" cried the twins, as they quickly found Shawn's name and then went back to looking for Amanda's.

All Amanda saw was a sea of names. Her heart sunk into her stomach as she looked up and down.

"It's not here," she muttered. She looked at Shawn in a panic. "Is my name here?" she asked.

Shawn looked up at the list so she wouldn't have to look at Amanda. "No," she said simply. She shook her head. "Oh, I wish you could have been with me! We would've had so much fun!"

Molly, who was behind Amanda, put her hand on Amanda's shoulder.

Just then, Amanda was jostled by someone. She turned around, and it was Angie. Angie was so tall that she'd seen her name over the crowd's heads. "There I am!" cried Angie, pointing to her name. "Angie Martinez!"

Angie turned to Shawn, and gave her a high five, practically over Amanda's head, as if Amanda wasn't even there. "You go, Shawn, you made it, too! We're the only two sixth-graders on the squad!"

"*Yessss!*" cried Shawn and Angie.

Amanda slunk out of their way. For a moment, she felt like she couldn't see. She reached for Molly, who murmured, "Let's go, Manda," and quickly led her down the hall. Amanda looked down, not wanting people to see that she was upset. When Amanda looked back, Shawn seemed to be a million miles away, huddled with Angie, who was saying in a loud voice, "See you at practice, Shawn!"

Lunch that afternoon was weird.

Everyone was happy for Shawn, and Amanda tried to be happy for her, too. But she felt as if something had changed. Something between Shawn and her? Something inside herself? She wasn't sure. "So, um, when do you start practice?" she asked Shawn.

Shawn was sitting back in her chair, relaxed and confident.

40

"Today after school!" said Shawn. "We've got our first football game in two weeks."

"Wow," said Natasha. "That's pretty soon."

"Our first football game" echoed in Amanda's ears. Shawn already seemed so...in the mix, so much a part of something. Something that Amanda wouldn't know anything about, now. Suddenly, Amanda felt five years old.

"Shawn!" cried a shrill voice. "I'll see you later, girlfriend."

It was Angie. She was standing up at her table, chewing a wad of gum, her hand on her hip, not caring that she attracted attention. She didn't even seem to notice Amanda and the rest of the girls.

Shawn smiled and waved back.

Just then, the bell rang, and Amanda was never so glad to get to math class. When she opened her textbook, a note was stuck inside. Amanda smiled. She knew it was from Molly, who'd probably put it there the night before. She opened the piece of pink paper.

Manda—no matter what happens with cheerleading, REMEMBER, you're awesome! You are going to have a GREAT year! You're the best!

xoxox Molls

41

It felt strange to walk home from school that afternoon without Shawn. Molly, Peichi, and Natasha all talked and joked, but Amanda was quiet.

Shawn could've been a little less happy in front of me, thought Amanda. *I can't believe how she carried on with Angie! Like I wasn't even there—I felt like a total geek!*

"So let's study at my house tomorrow," Amanda heard Peichi say. "Since we all have the same social studies textbook..."

Amanda's thoughts continued to race on. *Oh, well—I guess Shawn was just really excited. I just can't believe I'm not going to be a cheerleader. It's so not fair!*

"Amanda and I can come over at four thirty, after our piano lessons," Molly was saying, jarring Amanda out of her thoughts. "Right, Manda?"

"Uh-huh," said Amanda, before her thoughts took over again. She pictured herself at the football games, watching Shawn shine down there on the field, feeling like she was wearing a sign on her back that announced, I'M AMANDA MOORE, SIXTH-GRADE GEEK. I DIDN'T MAKE CHEERLEADING BUT MY GOOD FRIEND DID! *I'm so embarrassed that I didn't make it. Nothing's going to feel normal now. What's with that Angie girl? And what's so great about middle school, anyway?*

The following Sunday was chilly and wet. Amanda was breaking an egg into a bowl, listening to the rain, when Matthew slid into the kitchen in his socks, stopping only when he hit the counter.

"Doesn't that hurt?" asked Amanda.

"Nope. Where is everyone? I'm bored. What are you making?"

"Well, Dad's taking a nap—what else is new? Mom's in the den, reading. Molly's doing homework. And I'm making brownies 'cause the Chef Girls are coming over soon. We're having a business meeting."

"*Mmmm!* Brownies! Can I help?" asked Matthew.

Amanda sighed. So much for the peace and quiet she was hoping to find alone in the kitchen. But she smiled at her freckle-faced brother. She was trying to be nicer to him lately.

"Sure you can help. I'm going to try something new— mint icing for the brownies," Amanda replied.

"*Ugh!* Mint icing? Why can't you just make regular icing?" complained Matthew, wrinkling his nose.

"Mint icing's good. Take it or leave it."

"Okay. What do you want me to do?"

"Wash your hands," said Amanda.

"But they're not dirty," protested Matthew.

"Wash them anyway."

Cooking with her little brother was actually kind of nice. Amanda had to admit he tried hard to be a big help.

"You know what? This is gonna taste good," said Matthew later, as he tasted the icing. The brownies were about to come out of the oven.

"*Mmm.* Yeah, I think it will," said Amanda, nodding her head. "Thanks for helping me. I'll save some brownies for you, okay?"

"Thanks," said Matthew.

Just then, the doorbell rang.

"Okay, Matthew, my friends are here. Time to leave," Amanda said.

"Don't forget about the brownies," Matthew told her.

"I won't."

"Mmmm, it smells good in here," Peichi said as she walked into the kitchen.

Natasha and Shawn followed behind her.

"Hey, Molls!" Amanda shouted. "Everyone's here!"

"So guess *what!*" announced Peichi when Molly had come downstairs. "I now have my own phone! It's white and cordless, and it's right by my bed!"

"Wow," said all the girls enviously.

"Can we put your number on our business card?"

asked Molly. "People seem to always call here, but if we have two numbers, that might be better."

"I'll have to ask my mom," said Peichi.

"What's this meeting about, again?" asked Shawn, reaching for a brownie.

"To talk about Dish, and write down what we want on our business card," Molly reminded her. "The big question is, now that we're in school, what are we going to do about the business?"

"Well, I'm really busy now with cheerleading," said Shawn. "I don't think I'll have much time for Dish. And Grandma Ruthie's really strict with me. She goes over my homework with me and makes me do stuff over and—"

"These brownies are so good!" exclaimed Peichi. "Wow! We have to make these for our clients! Anyway, I'm really busy, too. Especially since I'm learning to speak and write Chinese after school. Can I have some more milk? Plus, I got straight A's last year, and I want to keep it up! *Mmm!* I love these brownies! Amanda, you're awesome!"

Peichi took another bite, which kept her quiet for the moment.

"I'm going to be busy, too," Natasha said softly. "With homework, plus Hebrew school. And the paper, which I think I'll join. I'm going to the first meeting. Unless I chicken out! But I think it could be fun."

"It would be cool to see your name at the top of an article," Molly told Natasha. Molly looked around the table. "Dish is doing really well now," she said. "Maybe we can try to cut back our work hours."

"It'll be hard to say good-bye to all that money we were making!" Peichi pointed out. "But it was our summer job."

Molly frowned. "Is that what it is for you guys?" she asked. "Just a summer job?"

"Well, Molls, we all agreed with our parents that it was a summer thing, and then we'd see what happened after that," Amanda reminded her.

"How about if we just do one or two jobs a month?" Molly asked the girls.

"Sounds good," said Shawn. "That's all I could handle. So, then, what do we need a business card for?"

"Because it's the professional thing to have," said Molly. "It's, you know, cool! It makes us look like a real business."

"Yeah! We'll tape it to the bags when we deliver food," said Peichi. "We'll give each customer more than one. Then they can keep one and pass on the other one."

"Whoops! I have to get going," said Shawn, checking her watch.

"Where do you have to go?" asked Amanda with a frown. "I thought we were going to hang out today."

"Um, I have to meet Angie," replied Shawn, as she looked around in her bag for something.

"Oh," said Amanda and Molly at the same time. They both tried to hide their disappointment.

"It's a cheerleading thing," said Shawn casually. She stood up. "We have to meet with the team about a charity fundraiser we'll be doing," she said, looking at Amanda. "No big deal."

"On a Sunday?" blurted Peichi.

"Yeah, on a Sunday," said Shawn, a little annoyed. "Okay? I gotta go."

"Sure," said Amanda. She forced a smile. "That s—sounds like fun."

"But you just got here, and we haven't thought of the wording for our card," protested Molly.

"I'm sure you guys will come up with something really great!" said Shawn, as she walked through the kitchen doorway. "I'll like whatever it is. Well, see ya."

"Bye," said everyone. Seconds later, they heard the front door close.

"Well!" said Amanda in a cheerful voice. She tried to put Angie out of her mind, but her mind raced. *Does Shawn like Angie more than Molly and me now? Did she really have to leave early?*

Everyone was looking at Amanda.

Amanda cleared her throat. "Well, anyway, let's figure out what we want to say on our business card. Then Peichi will give it to her mom, and she'll design the card for us." Mrs. Cheng was an artist and a graphic designer.

"Right," said Peichi. She gave Amanda a smile, which meant, *Don't worry, everything's gonna be okay!* "She'll design it for free of course," Peichi went on. "But we have to pay for the printer to make the cards. It'll come out of the money in the treasury." Peichi was the treasurer of Dish.

Everyone fell silent, thinking about the right words to describe Dish.

"What about, 'Are you tired of cooking?'" suggested Molly.

"Or, 'Too tired too cook?'" offered Natasha.

"Oh, that's better!" exclaimed Molly, reaching for her pen.

"Maybe we should put down that the food is home cooked. Because you can always get take-out when you're too tired," Amanda said.

"Good idea," Molly replied. "And we should put that we deliver!"

That's when Mr. Moore walked into the kitchen, his hair rumpled from his long nap. "Hello girls," he said. His blue eyes twinkled from behind his glasses. "Mind if I have a snack? Is anyone going to eat that brownie?"

"Go ahead," Amanda said. "But don't touch the ones over there," she said pointing to a yellow ceramic plate. "Those are for Matthew. I promised I'd save him some."

"What are you girls doing? Studying?" Dad asked. He wiped a brownie crumb off his lip. "*Mmm*. These are great!"

Molly quickly explained what they were doing and

read their line out loud. "Home cooking! Delivered to your door—when you're TOO TIRED to cook!"

"That sounds pretty good," said Dad. "But these days people aren't just too tired to cook—they're too busy."

"Oh!" said Molly. "That's even better." She changed the line and read it aloud.

"It sounds great," replied Mr. Moore.

"Super!" said Peichi. "Then it's ready to give to my mom. But let's put all of our names on the card first!"

"That type looks cute, Mom," said Peichi later that day. She was in her mom's office, watching her work on the computer. They'd tried a few different typefaces and had finally found the perfect look.

Mrs. Cheng smiled at the screen. "I like it, too," she said, tucking her sleek black bobbed hair behind her ear. She added some clip art she had on file—a chef's hat and a tiny tray of cakes.

Peichi loved watching her mom work. When Mrs. Cheng was finished, the card looked so cool and fun.

"Let's check the spelling and the phone number one more time," said Mrs. Cheng. "Then I'll e-mail it right to the printer, and we can probably pick up the cards later this week!"

"I can't wait to show it to the Chef Girls!" said Peichi. "Thanks, Mom!"

Amanda groaned the next morning as she walked down the main hall with Molly and Peichi. *When is someone going to take down those lists of who made cheerleading?* she thought.

But today there was something new tacked up over part of the cheerleading list.

"Look, you guys," said Amanda. Peichi and Molly stopped chatting to read the big sign.

"Wow," said Amanda. "I didn't know this school did musicals. That sounds like fun." She pictured herself singing on stage under the bright lights, wearing the long dress and big hat, being someone else.

"Be prepared to sing," read Peichi. "Can you guys sing?"

"No," said Molly.

"Sure," said Amanda at

the same time. The twins looked at each other and laughed.

"I like to sing," said Peichi. "I'm pretty good."

Suddenly Amanda wanted to be onstage in that dress more than anything, even more than she'd wanted to be a cheerleader. *But can I do it?* she wondered. *Can I get through another tryout? What if I make a complete idiot of myself again?*

Then again, she thought, *maybe I* won't *make a complete idiot out of myself.*

"Let's try out!" blurted Amanda.

"No way!" objected Molly. "I could never do something like that. It's way too scary."

"I'll do it! Why not?" said Peichi.

"Great!" said Amanda. "Molly, are you *sure* you don't want to?"

"Uh-huh, I'm sure," said Molly, as Amanda and Peichi wrote their names and grade on the sign-up sheet. "But I'll go with you and watch!"

For the next few days, Amanda found it hard to concentrate in class and on her homework. She kept wondering what the audition would be like. She pictured herself alone in the music room with the pianist and the director of the play, singing her heart out. Then the director would say, "Thank you, Amanda, you have real talent."

Or she'd be wearing a long dress, taking a bow at the end of the play. Mom and Dad and Molly and Matthew and the Chef Girls would be in the center row, on their feet clapping and cheering. And Justin would be there, too. She'd be a part of the school, part of something big. Just like Shawn.

I have to make this play, thought Amanda, *or I'm just gonna die!*

Then suddenly it was Thursday afternoon and time for the audition. Amanda told herself she wasn't nervous, but her heart was racing, her arms and legs were stiff, and her stomach felt tight. Earlier in the day, Peichi had passed her a note in English class:

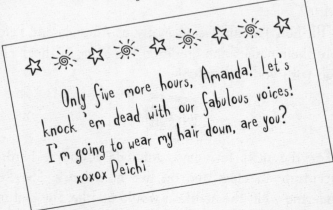

☆ ☀ ☆ ☀ ☆ ☀ ☆ ☀ ☆

Only five more hours, Amanda! Let's knock 'em dead with our fabulous voices! I'm going to wear my hair down, are you? xoxox Peichi

"Here goes!" said Peichi with her usual cheerfulness

as she and the twins approached the auditorium where lots of other kids were filing in.

"Aren't you nervous, Peichi?" asked Amanda.

"Nope," said Peichi. "This is gonna be fun!"

The auditorium was filled with the shouts and chatter of about a hundred kids, all nervously waiting for the audition to begin. A student handed out sheet music for a song from the musical.

Amanda looked up at the stage. A large piano was there.

"Oh, no!" she cried. "We have to sing up there? On the stage? In front of everyone?"

"Well, where did you think you were going to sing?" asked Peichi.

Just then, a tall, attractive, dark-haired woman walked into the auditorium and stood in front of the stage.

I've seen her before, thought Amanda.

"Hello and welcome, students!" she said. "I'm so *glad* you're all here for the *audition!* I'll be directing *My Fair Lady.* My name is Ms. Barlow—"

"Ms. Barlow," whispered Amanda to Molly and Peichi. "That's Brenda Barlow! What's *she* doing here?"

"*Ohmygosh!*" whispered the girls.

"For those of you who don't know me yet, I teach eighth-grade French, and I'm the drama coach here at Windsor Middle School," Ms. Barlow was saying. "I'm *also* an actress! Now let's get started. This is Mr. Cummings, Windsor's music teacher and choir director. He'll be accompanying us on the piano and teaching us a song from the musical. Then you'll come up to the stage to sing a few bars. We'll go in alphabetical order, starting with the eighth-graders. The cast list will be posted in the main hall tomorrow morning."

At least we get to go last, thought Amanda. *Maybe the older kids will have gone home by then...I can't believe Ms. Barlow works at our school!*

Recently, Ms. Barlow had hired Dish to do a dinner for her little girl's birthday. She'd been a difficult customer—she'd called several days before the event, but then called again and asked them to do it earlier in the week. But the Chef Girls had already committed to another cooking job for that same day.

Amanda had told her it was impossible, but Ms. Barlow had made such a fuss that Amanda agreed to the job just to get off the phone. And then, when the girls delivered the food, Ms. Barlow didn't have the money to pay them! It took a few days—and a note to remind her that was written by Natasha's dad—to get their money.

Everything had worked out in the end. Ms. Barlow had finally paid them and had been very gracious, but now Amanda was uneasy. *I hope she doesn't hold that note against me,* thought Amanda. *But she just might.*

Peichi, of course, wasn't giving it a second thought.

Amanda and Peichi learned a lot by watching the seventh- and eighth-graders audition. It was obvious who'd been in the school plays before—they moved easily on the stage and joked with Ms. Barlow. They faced the audience and sang with feeling. Tiffany Hurst, a tall eighth-grader who was one of the first to audition, seemed to own the stage.

"Oh, Tiffany's a triple threat," Amanda heard someone behind her telling her friend. "She'll probably get the leading role."

"What's a triple threat?" asked the friend.

"You know, someone who can act, sing, *and* dance."

Some students had terrible auditions. They acted nervous, hiding behind their sheet music. They were impossible to hear. Some kids weren't even standing up straight.

"We can't just sing the song," Amanda whispered to Peichi. "We have to sing it like we're already performing the play. And we can't show that we're nervous!"

"You're right," said Peichi, nodding.

Soon it was the sixth-graders' turns.

"Peichi Cheng!" called Ms. Barlow.

"*Oooh!*" whispered Peichi as she jumped out of her seat.

Amanda grabbed her hand. "Good luck, Peichi!"

Peichi practically bounced down the aisle and up the steps to the stage. She greeted Mr. Cummings, who murmured a few words to her, and then Peichi faced the audience with a big smile.

"So far, so good!" Molly whispered to Amanda.

Still wearing her big smile, Peichi started to sing. A few students giggled.

"*Ohmygosh!*" whispered Amanda. "She's terrible!"

Peichi was *way* off key—and completely clueless about it! She sang loudly and with expression, but her flat voice was almost painful to listen to.

"She sounds like a sick cat," giggled someone behind the twins.

"Thank you so *much!* That'll do, darling," cut in Ms. Barlow. "Thanks a *lot!*"

"Oh, okay!" said Peichi. "Thank you!" She quickly walked off the stage and back up the aisle, beaming.

For a moment, Molly couldn't think of anything to say. "Uh, good job!"

"Yeah, I could hear you really well," added Amanda. *What else can I say?* she thought.

"Thanks!" said Peichi. "That was fun! Oh, I hope I make it!"

Soon Amanda heard Ms. Barlow say, "Amanda Moore!"

Molly squeezed her hand, and as everyone turned to see who she was, Amanda walked carefully down the aisle, hoping she wouldn't trip.

"Hello, Amanda," said Ms. Barlow with a sincere smile. "*Nice* to see you again! Will you need sheet music, or do you have the song memorized?"

"Um, I'd better take it," Amanda heard herself reply. Her own voice sounded far away. She walked up the steps to the stage as if in slow motion.

Mr. Cummings gave her a nice smile, too. "Ready?" he said.

"Thank you, I mean, yes," said Amanda, confused. Mr. Cummings played the introduction.

As he played, Amanda remembered to stop looking at Mr. Cummings and look out at the audience. She tried to find Molly in the back, but couldn't.

Here goes, she thought, coming into the song right on time.

At first Amanda could barely hear her own voice. She began to sing louder, and heard that she was a little off-key. She quickly found the right key and began to smile and relax.

"Someone's head restin' on my knee...oh, wouldn't it be loverly..." The piano music seemed to be filtering into her muscles and helped her feel less alone on the stage. That's when she had the courage to look at the students in the first row. They were watching her— without laughing!

Amanda began to loosen up. She felt that the words to the song belonged to her, and almost believed that she was Eliza Doolittle, the main character in the play. She had a glimpse of what it must be like to perform on stage. It felt awesome!

And then it was over.

Mr. Cummings had stopped playing, and Ms. Barlow was saying, "Thank you, Amanda! Good job."

"Thank you!" said Amanda to Mr. Cummings. She quickly walked off the stage, flashed Ms. Barlow a smile, and then walked back up the aisle, trying to look casual.

"Yay, Amanda!" said Peichi.

"Way to go, Amanda!" said Molly, raising her hand for a high-five. "You were really good!

"Thanks, I think I did okay!" said Amanda. "Look at my hands! I'm shaking!" Amanda giggled. "Come on, let's go home."

That night, as Amanda and Molly were in their own bathroom getting ready for bed, Amanda said, "You know, Molls, this play is going to be a dinner theater. Maybe Dish should cater part of the dinner."

"Good idea," said Molly. "We should talk to Ms. Barlow about it."

While Amanda was in the shower, Molly went downstairs and sent an e-mail to all the Chef Girls.

To: qtpie490; happyface; BrooklynNatasha
From: mooretimes2
Re: Hi everyone!

It's Molls. The audition was cool. Tomorrow's the day that Amanda and Peichi find out if they will be big stars in *My Fair Lady!* Let's meet in the main hall as soon as we get to school and check out the cast list together! See ya in the morning!

"Wow, look at the crowd!" exclaimed Amanda the next morning.

"I think the whole school wants to find out who made it," observed Shawn.

Just then, the crowd parted as some students turned away. Peichi and Amanda squeezed up front.

"Oh! *Ohmygosh!* There I am!" cried Amanda, pointing to her name in the second column. "Wow!" She turned to grin at Molly and her friends, giving the "thumbs-up" sign. They shrieked.

"*Ooh*, Amanda, that's great!" said Peichi. "I don't see my name on here...." She kept looking. Amanda searched, too, but Peichi's name was not there.

"Oh, well," said Peichi. She shrugged and looked down at the floor.

Amanda put her hand on Peichi's shoulder. "Oh, Peichi, I'm sorry! I—"

"It's okay, Amanda!" insisted Peichi. Her old smile came back. "It's so exciting that you made it! You're practically the only sixth-grader! I just auditioned for fun." She and Amanda walked toward the girls. "It would be nice to still be involved in the play. I might do costume crew."

"Oh, good," said Amanda. "Then we'll still be in the play together."

That afternoon, Amanda went to the supermarket with Mom. As Molly was doing her homework in the kitchen, the phone rang.

"Hello, my name's Dawn Phillips. I live next door to Brenda Barlow," said the person on the line. "She told me all about Dish. I'm an intern at the hospital, and so is my roommate. We work long hours and don't have much time to cook. And we're tired of all the take-out food around here. We'd like to hire you to cook about three days' worth of food for us. We don't even care what it is, or what you charge us, as long as it's comfort food. Okay?"

"Uh, sure," said Molly. "No problem." *Comfort food?* she wondered. *What's that?* But she was too embarrassed to ask Dawn what it meant. *Maybe Amanda will know* she thought as she went back to her homework. Molly was writing an English essay when Amanda and Mom got home from shopping.

"Hi," said Amanda. She was holding a magazine.

"What's that?" asked Molly.

"*Celebrity Hairstyles.* I saw it at the store and asked Mom to buy it for me."

"So, guess what! We got another cooking job!" announced Molly.

"That's good."

"They want us to make comfort food. Do you know what that is?"

"I don't know," Amanda replied absently. She flipped through the magazine and played with her hair. "I wonder how my hair's gonna look in the play. I guess it'll be up, since I'll probably be wearing a really glamorous long dress."

Hello, thought Molly. *Do you even know I'm here?*

"So I hear you girls have another cooking job," said Dad at dinner. "Is this for a new client?"

"Uh-huh," said Molly. "It's for a couple of women who live next door to Brenda Barlow. They work at the hospital. They want us to make comfort food for them. But I don't know what that is. Do you?"

Dad smiled, and so did Mom.

"Comfort food is, well, food that makes you think of homey, comforting things," Mom tried to explain.

"It's food that you grew up with, that Mom or Grandma used to make," added Dad.

"You know what comfort food is to me? Mashed potatoes and gravy," Mom said with a laugh.

"*Mmm*, right," said Dad. "And fried chicken. Macaroni and cheese. Chocolate layer cake!"

"Shawn's grandma makes awesome fried chicken and mashed potatoes," Amanda suggested. "Maybe she could help us!"

"Girls, do you even have time to keep Dish running?" asked Dad. "I'm concerned about your schedules. You have homework and piano lessons. And now Amanda will be busy with the play."

Molly rolled her eyes.

"Remember, we said that Dish would just be a summer job, and then we'd see about it," added Mom.

"We talked about it with the Chef Girls," Amanda spoke up. "We're only going to do, like, one job a month. So this will be our one job."

Dad nodded.

"Okay," said Mom. "Just remember, your schoolwork has to come first."

"I can't wait to ask Shawn if Grandma Ruthie can help!" said Molly.

On Saturday, the twins, Natasha, Shawn, and Peichi all met up at Choice Foods, the local grocery store. Shawn brought the shopping list that Grandma Ruthie had written up, and Peichi brought money from the treasury to pay for it.

One of the things on Grandma Ruthie's shopping list was brisket of beef.

"I've never heard of brisket," admitted Molly.

"That's *sad!*" exclaimed Shawn. "You've been missing out your whole life! I ask her to make it for my birthday every year."

The next afternoon, everyone met at Shawn's apartment.

"Hello, hello," said Grandma Ruthie as the girls streamed in. "How are ya'll doing? Ready to cook?"

"Hel-*lo!* I'm Peichi!"

Shawn introduced Peichi and Natasha.

"Hi," said Natasha. "This is such a nice apartment." She looked around at the African tribal masks and a tall

64

wooden giraffe that Shawn's parents had brought back from Africa before she was born.

"Wow! Look at this view!" cried Peichi. She ran to the window, which overlooked Prospect Park. "Oops! I almost forgot! I have something very exciting to show you!"

"What is it?" asked Molly. "Our business cards?"

Peichi just smiled and pulled a package out of her backpack. It contained the cards, hundreds of them.

"*Oooh!*" cried everyone, gathering around.

"Wow! They look so good!"

"*Ohmygosh!* We're a real business now."

"It's so cool! Your mom did a great job, Peichi."

After everyone had inspected the cards and took some for themselves, Shawn announced happily, "My dad just called. Guess what! He's coming home early! He'll be here in a couple of days! I can't wait till he gets home."

"That's great, Shawn," said Amanda. She turned to Grandma Ruthie. "Are you going to stay for a while, or—"

"No, no, I'm going back to South Carolina," said Grandma Ruthie. "I like visiting New York for a bit, but it's always nice to go back home. Now step on into the kitchen, and let's get cooking. We've got a lot of work to do. Those young ladies want comfort food, and we're gonna give it to 'em, Southern style!"

The kitchen was a little crowded with six people in it, but the girls had a great time as they talked and laughed with Grandma Ruthie. The girls watched her fix the brisket that she'd marinated the night before. They helped make small buttermilk biscuits that she used as a topping for a chicken pot pie. They made the icing for yummy red velvet cake. They stirred the black-eyed peas.

"Not too much, now," Grandma Ruthie warned Peichi, as she reached for the wooden spoon. "You only need to stir these beans occasionally."

She smiled at the girls. "You know what comfort food means to me? Corn bread. With butter and honey on it. *Mmm, mmm.* Shawn, you've made corn bread with me before. Reach down in that cupboard for the cornmeal, and measure two cups of it into a bowl. Peichi, see how much buttermilk's left. Natasha, please beat two eggs for me."

Hours later, the girls carefully packed all the food and put it into boxes. Then they proudly taped their business cards on all of them.

"Dad said he'd drive us over to the client's house," said Amanda. "I'll call him to tell him we're ready."

"These ladies are going to be ve-ry happy!" predicted Peichi.

"I know," said Molly. "I wish this was going to be my dinner tonight!"

Shawn stopped and looked at her grandmother. "Grandma, what are *we* having for dinner tonight?"

"Chinese take-out! 'Cause Grandma's kitchen is closed for the evening," said Grandma Ruthie, and everyone laughed. "Girls, it was just great to see ya'll. I'll be leaving in a few days, so I think this is good-bye."

Fifteen minutes later, the girls filed up the steps of 126 Carroll Place and rang the bell. A petite young woman opened the door.

"Hi, I'm Dawn!" she said. "Come on in! I can't wait to see what you made for us!"

"I think you're going to like it," said Shawn, who was the first in the door.

"Something smells awesome!" said Dawn, leading the way down the hall.

"Oh, that's the barbecued brisket!" said Shawn. "And we have chicken pot pie—just bake it when you're ready to eat it. And black-eyed peas. And corn bread—"

"Wow!" exclaimed Dawn, as she greeted each of the girls coming down the hall. "You girls are *amazing!* My roommate is *not* going to believe this! We're from the

South, and this is going to make us feel like we're back home! This is comfort food, all right. Let me just get my pocketbook...."

Dawn disappeared into another room, and all the girls looked at one another. "We're good," said Shawn proudly.

"Here you go," said Dawn, reappearing. She handed Shawn a large bill.

"Oops," said Shawn, turning to look at the other girls. "We don't have any change."

"Keep the change," said Dawn. "You deserve it! How old are you girls, anyway?"

"Eleven," Molly spoke up.

"Eleven?" echoed Dawn, surprised. "I'm impressed."

"My grandma helped us a lot," said Shawn. "Well, thank you very much."

"Bye!" said all the girls, and they walked out the door.

"Good-bye," said Dawn with a wave. "I wish you could cook for us every week!"

Inside the car, Shawn flashed the big bill at Mr. Moore and the girls. "This is a lot of money!" she said. "Those ladies must be rich!" She handed the money to Peichi.

"I don't think they're rich," said Mr. Moore. "But they work really hard at the hospital, and they're probably just so grateful for some home-cooked food. Good job, girls!"

"Anyway, *we're* rich now," joked Peichi. "I'll break up

this bill when I get home, divide the money, and bring it back out to the car."

"That job went pretty well. Didn't it?" Molly asked the girls as they waited for Peichi.

"It sure did," said Shawn.

"Well, I was just thinking," Molly began. "Maybe we can take on another job. I know we said just one job a month, but..."

"No way," Amanda interrupted. "I'm going to be too busy. Rehearsals start tomorrow."

"And cheerleading practice takes up a lot of time," added Shawn.

"And I'm swamped, too," Natasha agreed.

Molly didn't say anything. She just sat there staring out the window, waiting for Peichi to come back downstairs.

8

The next day was the first rehearsal for *My Fair Lady*.

After school, Amanda was on her way to Ms. Barlow's clasroom, when she passed Peichi in the hall.

"Hi!" said Peichi. "Have a good rehearsal!"

"I can't wait to see what character I get to play!" said Amanda.

"I signed up for costume crew!" said Peichi. "And I'm going to our first meeting! We're going to find out what kinds of costumes we're going to make. See you later!"

Amanda waved, then turned down the hall to Room 23. It was a large classroom that had a small stage in it.

Cool, thought Amanda. Soon she'd be up there, rehearsing with the whole cast. She saw herself onstage, saying some clever line from the play, making everyone laugh. It felt so great to be involved in something. *Why wouldn't Molly want to do something like this?* she wondered, as she watched the other kids coming in. A pretty girl with long, curly, reddish-gold hair walked toward her. Amanda remembered her from the audition, and knew she was also a sixth-grader.

"Hi!" she said. "This is *My Fair Lady,* right?"

"Right," said Amanda. "I'm Amanda."

"I'm Tessa! You're in my third-period gym class, remember?"

"Oh," replied Amanda, "no, that's my twin, Molly. She has gym third period."

"You're a *twin?* That's so cool!"

Just then, the girls heard footsteps clicking down the hall, and Ms. Barlow made her entrance. "Hel-*lo,* everyone!" she called. "Welcome to the first day of rehearsal!" She patted a tall stack of paper. "Come get your scripts!"

"She looks like a movie star," whispered Tessa. Ms. Barlow was wearing high-heeled boots, a plum-colored skirt, and a black silk turtleneck. Her shiny dark hair looked beautiful against her pale skin, which was brightened with deep red lipstick.

Ms. Barlow passed around a cast list while everyone picked up a copy of the fat script.

"Wow!" said Amanda to Tessa. "My very own script. I *feel* like a movie star!" The girls giggled.

Someone handed Amanda the cast list, and she found her name. The list said:

AMANDA MOORE . . . . flower seller #4.

Flower seller number four? thought Amanda. *I don't even have a name?* She handed Tessa the list, then quickly flipped through the script. *I don't see any lines for the flower sellers. What if I don't even get to say anything?*

By the end of the week, Molly was having problems of her own. She was walking home from school on Friday with something in her backpack. It was only a few pieces of paper stapled together, but she could feel it weighing her down.

It was one of Miss Spontak's quizzes. Red pencil marks slashed through the numbers Molly had printed as she'd desperately tried to figure out the answers.

She'd barely gotten any of them right.

"Hi, sweetie, how was school?" asked Mom as Molly came in the door.

"Fine."

"Are you sure? Come out to the garden with me. We'll have a snack and take a look at your schoolwork together."

Molly forced a smile. "I—I'm just going upstairs to change my clothes." She headed upstairs to her bedroom and zipped open her backpack. She could barely look at the quiz with all those red marks.

She hesitated for a moment, then stuffed it under her bed. As soon as Amanda got home from rehearsal, she'd corner her.

"Amanda, will you help me with my math? It's so hard!" Molly asked.

"*Mmm-hmm,*" said Amanda in a faraway voice, flipping through her script. She looked up at Molly and sighed. "I'm only in a couple of scenes," she said. "I sing a few songs with everybody else, but I don't get to speak. Do you think Ms. Barlow would write me in a line if I asked her?"

"You'd really do that?" exclaimed Molly. She had to laugh. "That would take a lot of guts!"

Amanda giggled. "I know. Oh, I'd never do it."

Matthew suddenly appeared at the door.

"Yipes! You scared me," cried Molly.

"You're sneaking around again, Matthew," scolded Amanda.

"No, I'm not," insisted Matthew. "Guess what! We're going to Luigi's Restaurant for dinner! Mom says she doesn't feel like cooking tonight."

 "Yay!" cried the twins. They loved the big plates of spaghetti and meatballs at Luigi's. The twins grabbed their coats for the quick walk to the restaurant.

Just as the Moores began eating their dinner, Molly suddenly noticed a familiar figure sitting at a table for two in a far corner of the restaurant.

"Hey," said Molly, nudging Amanda, "there's Mr. Jordan. Way over there in the corner."

Amanda looked up from her plate. Mr. and Mrs. Moore glanced behind them.

"When did he get back from Australia?" asked Mom. She'd been friends with Shawn's dad since they had gone to high school together.

"Just a few days ago," replied Amanda. "Who's that lady with him? I've never seen her before."

"Is he on a *date?*" gasped Molly.

"Molly," said Dad in his low "warning" voice. Mom shot her "the look."

"Molly, stop shouting," said Matthew. "He'll hear you."

"*You* stop shouting," hissed Molly. "Is he on a date?" she repeated in a whisper.

Mom and Dad looked at each other and smiled. Their expressions seemed to say, *How about that!*

Mom looked at the twins. "Maybe he is, or maybe it's just a business dinner."

"Do people go on business dinners on Friday nights?" asked Amanda.

"Sometimes," said Dad. "Either way, it's not really *our* business, is it?" He smiled at the twins.

"I guess not," said Molly, looking down at her plate.

"I guess not," echoed Amanda, twirling her fork in her spaghetti.

"I guess not," said Matthew in a girly voice, imitating his sisters. His shirt was already splattered with tomato sauce.

Molly and Amanda couldn't help looking over at Mr. Jordan during dinner. His back was to the girls, but they were able to check out the attractive woman he was with. She wore a bright pink dress and seemed to laugh at everything Mr. Jordan said.

Where was Shawn? wondered the girls. And did she know what was going on?

As soon as they got home from Luigi's, Amanda picked up the phone.

"Hi, Shawn," said Amanda into the receiver.

"Hi!"

"Hi, Shawn, I'm here, too," said Molly on the extension. "What's up?"

"Oh, not much. I'm just hanging out here with Grandma Ruthie. She's been teaching me how to knit. She's going home tomorrow. Dad went out to dinner for a few hours and he just got back." The twins heard a muffled sound as Shawn turned her head away from the phone. "I'll be right there, Dad!" she called, then turned back to the phone. "What did you guys do tonight?" she asked the twins.

"We went to Luigi's for dinner," said Molly.

"We saw your dad there," said Amanda. "He didn't see us. He was kind of far away from us. Was he on a date?"

There was a pause.

"A *date?*" asked Shawn sharply. "I don't *think* so. Why would he go on a *date?* He said he was just going out to dinner with a friend."

"Oh, okay," said Amanda quickly. "Well, we'll talk to you later!"

"Bye," said Molly.

"Good-bye," said Shawn. Molly and Amanda could tell she was mad.

The twins hung up and looked at each other without saying anything.

"Uh, did we do something we shouldn't have?" Molly finally asked. "I sorta think we did."

Amanda frowned. "Shawn seemed kind of upset. Maybe we shouldn't have said anything." She sighed. "Oh, well, it's too late now to do anything about it. Anyway, don't you think her dad should have *told* her he was going on a date?"

"I don't know," said Molly. "Maybe he was going to tell her afterward and we blew it for him. Yipes! Or maybe it *wasn't* a date." Molly folded her arms over her chest and said glumly, "I guess Dad's right. It was really none of our business."

Monday after school, Shawn was at cheerleading practice. It was a hot day, and she was in a rotten mood. She didn't want to be at practice. All day, the only thing she'd wanted to do was be by herself, listening to music in her room. She hardly talked to the girls at lunch. Molly and Amanda hadn't looked her in the eye much. She knew they felt bad about calling her the other night. But she was glad they'd called, even though she didn't tell them so.

At least she was getting information.

What's up with Dad? she kept wondering. *Why does he have to date? How could he do that to Mom? And me?*

"Shawn, are you going to join us?"

Shawn suddenly snapped to attention. She looked up to see Coach Carson looking at her. Actually, the whole squad was looking at her questioningly, like, *Hello?*

"Sorry," said Shawn. She'd completely spaced out. What was she supposed to be doing?

"Shawn, I just announced that we're having an extra practice this week. Can you make it?" asked Coach Carson patiently.

"Oh, sure," said Shawn. "I'll be there."

"Okay," said Coach Carson. "Let's get in line and work on the new cheer. We've got a lot to do today."

After practice, Coach came up to Shawn as the girls were heading back to the locker room.

"Everything okay, Shawn?" she asked. She gave Shawn a warm, understanding smile. "You seem to have a lot on your mind today."

"Oh, everything's okay," said Shawn. She smiled back. "Thanks. Uh, sorry about spacing out earlier."

Whoa, she thought, *I must have been really out of it.*

"You're not eating that much," Mr. Jordan pointed out

at dinner that night. "Aren't you hungry? Better eat up, 'cause this is the last of the fried chicken your grandma made for us."

"Dad?" asked Shawn. "Who'd you go to dinner with on Friday night?" She gulped.

That had just slipped out. It was like she'd been thinking about it so much for the entire weekend that it had come out on its own.

Mr. Jordan's eyebrows shot up in surprise.

"Well," he said. He cleared his throat. He adjusted his glasses.

Here it comes, thought Shawn. Her heart started to pound. *Some kind of bad news!*

"I went to dinner with a woman named Donna Payne. She's very nice. I met her on the plane, coming home from Australia."

"Oh," said Shawn.

"We sat next to each other on the plane, and talked. It's a long flight, you know. So, anyway, I asked her if she'd like to have dinner with me. That's all."

"So it *was* a date!" cried Shawn. "Molly and Amanda were right!"

"Molly and Amanda?" asked Mr. Jordan, confused.

"The Moores were at Luigi's, too," explained Shawn. She felt a lump growing in her throat. "Oh, Daddy, how could you go on a date? What about Mom?" Tears blurred her vision. She felt her dad's hand on her shoulder.

"Baby," said Mr. Jordan kindly, "it was just a nice dinner with a nice person. You know what? I like to go to movies and go out to dinner and be with friends. Just like you do. Do you understand? Dads need to have fun, too."

Shawn nodded. That did make sense. But...

"Are you going to get married to Donna?" she asked sadly.

Mr. Jordan smiled and shook his head. "No, sweetie," he said. "I'm not thinking about getting married right now. But I do want to have a social life." He chuckled. "Donna was just here in New York on business anyway. The day after our dinner, she flew up to Boston to see her family. Then she flies back to Australia. I'll probably never see her again, but I enjoyed having dinner with her."

"I see," said Shawn.

"You'll always be the number one girl in my life," Mr. Jordan assured Shawn. "And you know how much I loved your mother. Just like you, I've been sad since she died. Neither of us will ever forget her."

"That's right, Daddy," said Shawn. "We never, ever will."

chapter 9

"**R**oom 303," Natasha muttered to herself on Monday after school. She was in an empty hallway, searching for the newspaper office. "Oh, here it is."

That's when Natasha hesitated. She wanted to go inside for the first newspaper meeting, but her feet refused to go any further.

Can I really do this? she thought. *What if I'm the only sixth-grader and no one talks to me?*

Just then, Justin came walking down the hall. "Hi, Natasha!" he said. "Are you going to the newspaper meeting?"

Natasha smiled, relieved to see someone she knew. "Yes, are you?"

"Yeah. I want to be on the photo staff. Come on, let's go in."

Justin and Natasha weren't the only sixth-graders, but there weren't many.

A petite, round, blond teacher came in and closed the door behind her. Smiling and showing a few dimples, she said, "Hello, I'm Ms. Zane. I'm the faculty advisor of <u>The Post</u>. Welcome to the meeting, everyone. This is a nice turnout! I'd like to introduce Lena Zagorski, who is editor-in-chief of <u>The Post</u>. And that's Brian Jones, photo editor. Lena, I'm going to turn it over to you!"

A tall girl with long, dark hair stood up. "Hi, everyone, thanks for coming today," she said. *She seems so confident,* thought Natasha enviously.

"Our first issue of <u>The Post</u> comes out in two weeks," Lena went on. "And I'd like to make this year's paper even better than last year—which will be a challenge since the paper was so awesome!"

"Yeah!" exclaimed some students.

Lena asked everyone what they were interested in doing, and the group divided into writers and photographers. Justin moved over to Brian's group.

"We've got a lot to cover," said Lena. "A lot of games are going on next week. And I want to start some special features."

Games? thought Natasha. *I don't want to be a sportswriter. Uh-oh! What if they make me write about the football game? I don't even know how to play football!*

"Who wants to cover this week's football game against Bay Ridge?" asked Lena. A couple of boys raised their hands.

"Tom, you can cover it. Garth, I'd like you to write a feature about Mr. Tafoya, the new football coach."

"Excellent!" said Garth.

"Now, for the girls' soccer game..." Lena's eyes searched the room.

"Natasha…" said Lena, thinking. She was looking down at her notes.

Everyone turned to look at Natasha. She could feel her cheeks burning.

"You can cover the soccer game," Lena told Natasha, "or you can interview a student that you find interesting. I want to feature a different student in every issue."

Interview? Talk to someone I've never met? Well, that is what a reporter does, Natasha told herself. *And I'm not that interested in soccer…*

"I'll do the interview," said Natasha quickly. She couldn't keep Lena waiting.

"Great!" said Lena. "Let me know your ideas by the end of the meeting. Then we'll brainstorm with Ms. Zane for a few minutes." Her gaze shifted to the girl next to Natasha. "You're Tanya, right? Would you like to cover the soccer game?"

"Sure," said Tanya.

Rats, thought Natasha. *Maybe I should've done soccer. What if I don't know what questions to ask in my interview? And how am I gonna come up with an idea by the end of this meeting? Too late now…*

Natasha only half-listened during the rest of the meeting. She was too busy trying to think of an interesting student to interview.

Suddenly, it hit her. *The Chef Girls! I'll interview the Chef Girls,* she thought. *About Dish!*

After the meeting, Ms. Zane and Lena came up to Natasha.

"So, Natasha, have you had a chance to think about whom you might interview?" asked Ms. Zane. She smiled. "I know we didn't give you much time."

"Um, I was thinking of more than one person, actually," said Natasha. She told Ms. Zane and Lena all about Dish.

"Sounds very interesting," said Ms. Zane.

"*Mmm-hmm,*" said Lena, nodding her head.

"There's only one little problem," said Ms. Zane. "Naturally, you'll want to interview all of the girls in Dish. But you're a part of Dish. As a journalist, you're supposed to be impartial—and you can't really interview yourself."

"Oh, right," said Natasha. "I hadn't thought of that."

"But is it such a big deal that Natasha's in Dish?" asked Lena. "This isn't a hard news story. It's a feature article on interesting students. She can mention that she's in Dish. But she'll let the people she's interviewing tell most of the story."

Ms. Zane grinned. "Okay, Lena, I'm convinced. Natasha, you can get started, and let us know if you need help. We'll want a photographer to take some pictures, too!"

"How about Justin?" asked Natasha. She pointed. "That kid over there. He's a friend of ours." She giggled. "Actually, he helped us with one of our cooking jobs when a couple of the other girls were grounded!"

Lena and Ms. Zane laughed. "Perfect!" said Ms. Zane.

"Great!" said Natasha. She picked up her backpack. "See you next week!" Walking out of the office, she suddenly felt important, more grown-up. She was a feature writer, with her own article in the paper. With her name on it!

"So, what do you think?" Natasha asked the Chef Girls the next morning on the walk to school. She'd just told them all about her writing assignment.

"I can't believe we'll be featured in the paper's first issue!" exclaimed Molly. "With a picture!"

"And guess who's going to take the picture?" asked Natasha. "Justin! He'll be working on the paper, too."

"Justin?" asked Amanda. "So you'll be working together. That's nice." But it didn't feel that nice to her. *Oh, well,* she thought. *I'm an actress now and I'm too busy to worry about those two.* "Did I tell you that Ms. Barlow said that I have a really great voice?" she said, changing the subject. "Yeah, she came up to me after rehearsal the other day and said that I project really well. That means the audience will hear me just fine..."

For all the girls, the next few weeks went by quickly. There were essays to write and lots of studying, quizzes, exams, and after-school activities.

Somehow, the girls managed to fit in a cooking job for Mrs. Freeman, who'd hired them before. Shawn didn't come, though. She said she was too busy with cheerleading. Amanda tried not to let it bother her, but she felt that she didn't even get to talk to Shawn much anymore. But she was having fun with the play, and she and Tessa were becoming friends. They'd rented *My Fair Lady* and watched it at Tessa's house.

One day at rehearsal, Ms. Barlow announced that it was time for everyone to be measured for their costumes. The costume crew came into the classroom.

Peichi rushed over to Amanda. "Hi!" she cried. "Guess what! I'm working on your costume! What a coincidence, huh? See? Ms. Barlow sketched what it'll look like." She showed a drawing of a woman in a long black skirt, a high-necked blouse, and a hat.

"*Hmmm,*" said Amanda. "Right, this looks like what the flower sellers wore in the movie."

Peichi pulled some black fabric out of a bag. "Here's the material for the skirt. I'll tear it here and there so that it'll look old and raggedy, of course...see this old black shawl? We found it at the Salvation Army. You'll wear this over the skirt. And I think we already have an old blouse that will fit you, but then it doesn't really matter if it fits, does it! 'Cause you're a poor flower seller with a dirty face! We'll make the blouse look like it has soot on it. Isn't it great? It's been so much fun working on your costume!"

Amanda didn't say anything for a moment. "Uh," she finally said, "it *is* neat that you're working on my costume."

"Well, what do you think?" asked Peichi anxiously. A disappointed look flashed across her face. "Don't you like it?"

No, I don't! Amanda wanted to say. *This is so blah! No one is even going to see me under this big black skirt and big black shawl!*

Just then shrieks erupted across the room as Ms. Barlow unfolded a bolt of white netting with white polka dots to show some of the eighth-grade girls. "Isn't this *gorgeous?*" she was saying. "And look, here's some pink chiffon. This will look great for one of the evening dresses. And look at these big blue feathers! Perfect for the big hats you'll wear! Here are the white gloves..."

Wow, thought Amanda, *I wish I could wear something like that!* She turned to Peichi. Poor Peichi had been so excited, and Amanda didn't want to hurt her feelings. "I think my costume looks, uh, really great! Thanks, Peichi!"

"*Whew,*" said Peichi. Her face relaxed. "For a minute, I didn't think you liked it! I couldn't believe I found this old black shawl! We had so much fun that day with Ms. Barlow at the Salvation Army..."

I've got to get a better-looking costume, Amanda was thinking as Peichi chattered on. *I've just got to!*

Amanda sighed a lot that night at dinner.

"Is something the matter, Manda?" asked Mom.

"Oh, not really." Amanda sighed again. She looked up and everyone was looking at her as if to say, *Well? What is it?*

Amanda set down her fork. "It's just that—well—it's so terrible."

"*What?* What's terrible?" asked Matthew. He pretended to choke himself, making his eyes bug out. "You look okay to me."

"It's not funny, Matthew," Amanda said. "This is about my *costume*. It's not right. Peichi is working on it, and I can't hurt her feelings! But it's so blah!"

"But sweetie, your costume's supposed to be plain," said Mom patiently. "You're a flower seller."

"Make that flower seller number four," said Amanda with a pout.

Matthew and Molly giggled, and Amanda's face turned red. "Why? Why does it have to be plain? What can't I look good? No one's even going to notice me! I want to stand out and look important! This is my first play! And I'm not cool in it! I'm just not cool."

"Look, sweetie," began Mom. "Every role in the play is important. The play wouldn't work if it had just glamorous people in it. The whole point is that Eliza Doolittle goes from being a poor flower seller to an elegant lady. Well, you're one of her flower-seller friends. You're plain. That's your job. But you're also singing in it, and dancing! That's exciting! Wait and see—when the whole play comes together, you'll feel *very* important. Trust me!"

"And remember, you're supposed to be trying something new and having fun," added Dad. "You *are* having fun, aren't you?"

Amanda nodded. "Yes, I am. But..."

"Gee, Amanda," said Matthew. "You sure have a lot of problems that aren't really problems."

Amanda pretended she didn't hear him.

That night, Amanda called Peichi.

"Hi!" said Peichi. "Are you studying for the English test?"

"Uh-huh," said Amanda. She cleared her throat. "But I'm calling about the play. I mean my costume."

"Oh! What's up? Do you want to see what I've done to

it? Stop by the costume room tomorrow after school. I'll be there."

Amanda winced. "It's just that I think it needs a little—something," she said. "You know, a little color, maybe a little more shape?"

"I don't think so," said Peichi.

"Give me a minute," pleaded Amanda. "Don't worry, I've thought it all out. Ms. Barlow told us to think up stuff about our characters' personalities and lives and stuff, so that it will help us act out the part and make it believable. Well, this is what I made up about my character: she used to be really rich! And her husband died of a terrible sickness that was going around London. And so then she didn't have any money, because in those days ladies didn't work, of course, but at least she still had her beautiful clothes, so she wears those when she sells flowers! Doesn't that sound good?"

"Well," said Peichi, "I guess. But—"

"I mean, we can take a pretty dress and make it look kind of old, like she's been selling flowers in it for a year," Amanda continued. "But it can still look elegant. What do you think? I think it's such a cool idea. I mean, you're doing such a great job, but I'm just thinking that we should have some variety."

"But Amanda," said Peichi. She was starting to get angry. "I mean, your costume is almost finished. And we're starting on the more complicated stuff, like the

89

elegant dresses for the horse race at Ascot, as well as the ball. I'm supposed to help decorate all the big hats."

"Well," said Amanda. "Can't you just ask Ms. Barlow, at least? I've got it all figured out. Just say to her, 'Ms. Barlow, I've been thinking, all the flower sellers look alike. Why don't we make one of them look like a lady who wasn't *always* a flower seller? She'd wear something a little more elegant.'"

"I don't know," said Peichi. She cleared her throat. *Why is Amanda doing this to me?* she thought. *I did such a great job on her costume.*

"Oh, just try it," said Amanda with a little laugh. "It's not a big deal. I'll help you! Okay, repeat after me: 'You know, Ms. Barlow, I've been thinking, all the flower sellers look alike.'"

Peichi rolled her eyes. "Amanda, I really have to get back to studying now."

"Oh, okay," said Amanda. "I'll see you tomorrow! Bye."

As Peichi hung up the phone, she thought, *What's with this "Repeat after me?" Yeah, right, like I'm gonna ask Ms. Barlow if we can change Amanda's costume! Who does she think she is anyway?*

chapter 10

"Flower sellers," called Ms. Barlow at the start of the next rehearsal. "I'm making some changes to the script." She passed around some stapled sheets of paper. "The play is running too long," she explained. "I'm cutting a scene— so I needed to write in some lines for you, to help bridge the scene I'm cutting. Please practice together while I work with the leads up on the stage. I'll be back later to hear your lines—and your working-class British accents!"

Amanda and Tessa looked at each other and said, "Yesss!" They quickly gathered with the two other girls playing flower sellers.

"Hey, look!" said Tessa, pointing to the first page. "There you are, Flower Seller Number Four! And here I am, Flower Seller Number Two."

"Wow, I have one, two, three, four lines!" said Amanda, as her eyes scanned down the page. "Cool! I'm glad I've been practicing the funny accent! Don't forget, we have to drop our 'H's'."

"That's not 'awd to do!" Tessa said in the accent.

" 'Ey, your accent is not 'alf bad." Amanda giggled. She loved talking that way.

Having lines to speak made Amanda feel a lot better,

but it made her want to change her costume more than ever. After rehearsal, Amanda hung around until all of the students had left.

"Ms. Barlow? Can I ask you a question?" said Amanda.

"Oh, sweetheart, I'm running, *run*-ning to pick up my little darling from the sitter," she said, "but if you walk *very* quickly down the hall with me, I'll be happy to chat! Now, what's on your mind?"

"Oh, okay," said Amanda, her heart sinking. She'd wanted a heart-to-heart chat with Ms. Barlow, sitting down with plenty of time to tell her how the costume just didn't work.

Here goes, thought Amanda. "Well, it's about my costume," she said.

"Oh, your costume!" said Ms. Barlow, brightening. "Isn't it *wonderfully* dreary? So black! So heavy!"

"*Um—*" said Amanda. This wasn't going the way she'd planned.

"Wait till you see the little black work boots we found for you at the Goodwill! Oh, they're perfect! Now, what did you want to ask me about it?"

"Well, don't you, um, think that it's a little *too* dark?" asked Amanda. "I mean..." She was out of breath now, Ms. Barlow was walking so fast. "I just think maybe it doesn't go with the character I made up in my head, the one you told us to think about. I made up that my character used to be rich, and so I think I need, you know, a little more

92

color—?" Amanda didn't even know what she wanted to ask for anymore. Her head was spinning and all she could hear was Ms. Barlow's heels—*click-clack-click-clack!*

"Ah, color! Don't worry, dear, the flowers you carry in your basket will add color. There! Problem solved! Bye-*bye!*"

"Bye," said Amanda. *That's that. Oh, well, at least I have some lines now!*

When Molly got home from school that day, Mrs. Moore was waiting for her with a glass of lemonade—and some crumpled papers on the kitchen table.

Crumpled papers with red marks all over them. The last two math quizzes.

"Oh. Hi." Molly stopped. Her feet felt like they were glued to the floor.

"I found these under your bed when I washed your sheets," said Mrs. Moore. "Molly, you said you were doing fine in school. Why didn't you tell me you were having trouble in math?"

Molly didn't say anything. She shifted uneasily, then stared down at her sneakers. "I don't know. I guess I thought you'd be mad."

"I'm not mad, Molly, but I am concerned. You've never had poor grades before. I can tell that you're falling behind. You can't just stuff your bad grades under your bed and hope they'll go away."

Mrs. Moore patted the chair next to her. "Come here, have some lemonade, and let's talk. I thought you and Amanda did your homework together. She's not having trouble in math."

Molly shook her head. "We used to do our homework together, but now we have different teachers, remember? So we have different homework. And Amanda gets impatient sometimes. She's helped me a little. But..."

"I see," said Mom. "Oh, the phone rang a little while ago, and it was a woman who wants you girls to cook for them."

"Really?" said Molly. "Someone new?"

"Yes, a new client. But I gave her the Cheng's number. I told her that you were unavailable for this job."

"Why, Mom?"

"Molly, I think you know the answer to that question. I'm afraid that until your grades come up, Dish is going to have to take a backseat in your life. I'm not going to let you fail math. And Amanda's got her hands full, too. Understand?"

Molly nodded. "Yes, I understand. But that's, like, the only time we get to see everyone now. Since everyone's so busy. And I doubt that Peichi and Natasha and Shawn

94

are going to want to do it without us. That'll be bad for business!"

But Mom's mind was made up. Dish was out, at least for now.

Great, thought Molly. *Now all I have is schoolwork and piano lessons.*

Molly and Mrs. Moore spent the rest of the afternoon going over Molly's quizzes and her homework for the evening. Just as they were finishing up, Amanda walked in the door from rehearsal. The phone rang.

Amanda grabbed the phone as she walked through the kitchen.

"Hello? Oh, hi, Natasha, what's up?" A few moments later, she handed Molly the phone. "Natasha wants to talk to both of us," she explained. "I'll get on the other line."

"Can I take it, Mom?" asked Molly.

"Go ahead," said Mom. "But you and I are going to do some more work after dinner. I want to make sure you really understand this."

"Hi," said Natasha after the twins got on the phone. "I'm calling to see when I can interview you both for my article. It would be nice to get all the Chef Girls together at the same time. How about tomorrow at lunch?"

"Sure," said Molly and Amanda at the same time.

"Good," said Natasha. "Well, see you in the morning."

"Oh," said Molly, "a new client called here earlier, but Mom gave them Peichi's number. I guess Peichi will call you. Mom's not allowing Amanda or me to do Dish for a while. So you and Peichi and Shawn will have to do the job without us, if you want it."

"Really?" asked Natasha, surprised.

"Really?" asked Amanda. She looked at Molly. "Why?"

"I'll tell you later," said Molly.

"I have to get going, anyway," said Natasha. "You know how my mom is—she doesn't want me to be on the phone too long. Oh, one more thing. Justin will call you about when he's going to take our picture."

"Great!" said Amanda. "Bye."

"Bye."

Seconds later, the phone rang again.

"Hello?" said Amanda. Her face reddened. "Oh, hi, Justin!...You want to take our picture for Natasha's article, right?" She giggled. "Natasha told us you'd be calling. So, when should we do it?...Oh, it has to be tomorrow?...Yeah, our kitchen would be the best place to take it...Great. We'll have some food out so that it'll look like we're cooking. See you tomorrow at eight. We'll tell the others. Bye."

That night, as Mom and Molly went over math problems, Amanda finished studying for her science quiz, then practiced her lines in front of the mirror.

"Why, I 'awven't seen Eliza Doolittle in many a week! She's a fawncy lady now. She's forgotten all about us, she 'as!"

I'm good at this! thought Amanda. *I'm a good actress...Let's see, what's the best way to pose? Maybe Justin will take a picture of me in the play, too. I'll become a big star and Justin will be a famous photographer. He'll take all my publicity photos for the magazines...*

Later, when Molly came upstairs, Amanda cried, "Molls! Help me learn my lines."

"Help me learn my math," muttered Molly.

"Later, okay? Here's the script. Now you say the line before mine, and then I'll say my line. Get it?"

"Well, duh, it's not that hard to figure out, Manda," retorted Molly. She scanned the script. "Which flower seller are you?"

"Number four. Okay, ready? Go ahead."

"Okay," said Molly. "Blimey? Where's Eliza Doolittle been lately?" She put down the script and giggled. "What does 'blimey' mean?"

"It's just an expression that they used to say in England," said Amanda. "Maybe they still do."

"You don't know what it means, do you!"

"Anyway, Molly, your accent is all wrong. Say it with the accent. It'll be a lot more fun. Say it like this: bluymee!"

But hearing that made Molly crack up, and then she was useless to Amanda.

The next day at lunch, the girls met up with Natasha.

"Guess what!" Natasha said to the twins and Peichi. She pulled a pen and a pad out of her bag. "After I turn in this article, I'm going to write an article about the play!"

"That's great! Make sure you put in something about flower seller number four!" Amanda said. "And you can interview me again, too!"

Molly rolled her eyes and changed the subject. "You really must like working on the paper. Did you have to talk your mom into letting you do it?"

Natasha shrugged. "No, she was actually cool about it. I never know what she's going to be cool about, or not. Anyway, I like going to the meetings and coming up with ideas for stories. I'll be coming to watch some rehearsals. With a photographer. Maybe Justin."

Amanda pictured herself on stage, saying her lines, and Justin snapping picture after picture.

"Anyway, here goes! My first interview!" said Natasha. "Chef Girls, what do you think of the cafeteria food? No, that's a joke. I'm not really putting that in there."

"Good," said Molly, "because there isn't much to say about it."

"Okay, seriously now," said Natasha. "Wait, where's Shawn? I thought I saw her heading over here."

The girls turned their heads. Shawn had been snagged by Angie. The girls tried to get her attention. Angie saw what they were doing, but she didn't bother to tell Shawn, who was facing away from them.

"Great," groaned Natasha. "Oh, well. I guess she forgot."

I'm not going over there to get her, thought Amanda. *No way.*

Natasha felt the same way. "I'll just have to interview her later," she said.

"Okay, ask us some questions!" said Peichi eagerly. "Interview us! Let's see you in action!"

Natasha laughed. "Okay. What do you like most about Dish?"

"That's easy," replied Molly. "It's so fun when we're all working in the kitchen together."

"I like figuring out what we're going to make for the client," said Peichi. "And then deciding who gets to work on what. And knowing we only have one day to do all the cooking!"

"I like delivering it to the clients, and seeing their faces when they open the box of our delicious food," said Amanda.

"*Ohmygosh!*" cried Peichi suddenly, checking her watch. "I forgot that I promised Ms. Barlow I'd come by the costume room for a few minutes at the end of lunch.

I have to hurry up and eat. But, Natasha, I'll see you tonight at the photo shoot and we can talk more. Okay?"

"Oh, okay," said Natasha. She looked disappointed.

"I'm sorry," said Peichi, as she quickly finished the last of her sloppy joe.

"Keep going," Molly said to Natasha.

"Okay," Natasha replied. "Um, do you consider Dish a success?"

Molly and Amanda looked at each other and giggled. "A success? That sounds so grown-up," said Amanda.

"But I guess you could say it is!" said Molly. "Because the first job we did made the client happy, and she told a friend about us. And some people have asked us to cook for them more than once."

"Good," said Natasha. "How do you decide what to cook?"

"Well," said Molly, "we pretty much cook the same stuff for most people. And it has to be food that will keep for a few days. Sometimes people have requests, and if we think we can do what they request, we will. But we've also told people that we don't know how to make certain things they want."

"Whose idea was it to have the business?" asked Natasha.

"It wasn't like someone said, 'Hey, let's have our own business,'" said Molly. "I was the one who wanted to cook dinner for our family one night, and it was our mom's idea to cook for our neighbors when their kitchen caught on fire."

"And it was my idea to start a cooking club," said Amanda. "Then Shawn thought of earning money cooking for busy people. So the idea just came together."

"Great!" said Natasha. "What are your plans for Dish?"

Molly sighed. "Well, as you know, I can't do Dish until my grades come up. And Amanda's too busy." Her eyes widened. "Natasha, you're not going to print that in the article, are you? The part about my grades?"

"Don't worry," said Natasha with a laugh. "I won't."

"And we turned down that customer that other day," Amanda reminded the girls.

"Right," said Natasha. "Without the two of you to help, and because we're all so busy now, Peichi, Shawn, and I didn't think we could do it."

Molly sighed. "Well, we'll probably never hear from her again. Anyway, I guess you could write that Dish is on the back burner for a few months while we adjust to school. Get it? 'Back burner'?"

"Ha ha," said Natasha and Amanda, rolling their eyes.

"Oh, I don't really have to say anything about that," said Natasha. "I'll just say that we only do it when we have time. Thanks! This was great. I only have a few days to write this." She grinned and added, "The paper's coming out this Friday! Can you believe it?"

"Really?" asked Amanda. "That's not much time." *I've*

never seen Natasha so excited about something, she thought.

"Yes, but that's like a real newspaper," Natasha pointed out. "Real reporters don't get much time. So I guess it's good experience. Well, see you tonight."

"Good luck!" said Molly.

"I can't wait to see your article," said Amanda. "It's so exciting for all of us! Oh, by the way, maybe you should just mention that I'm also in the cast of *My Fair Lady!*"

Gimme a break, thought Molly.

"Oh. Well, I'll think about it," said Natasha.

Later, as Molly and Amanda walked home from school together, Molly said, "Natasha seems different. In a good way."

"Yeah," said Amanda. "She seems happier...um, more—"

"Sure of herself," said Molly.

"Right, she's more sure of herself."

I wish I were feeling more like that, thought Molly. *I'd better get my grades up, fast.*

The photo shoot that night was a blast. The girls wore the chefs' aprons that they'd gotten for graduating from their summer cooking class.

"I think I'll take a few photos of you doing things

separately, and then a group shot," announced Justin. "Okay? Peichi, pretend to be chopping the onion... Natasha, stand here and measure the flour. Molly, you can operate the mixer. Amanda, pretend you're stirring something at the stove. Shawn, you can break an egg into a bowl."

Justin took several pictures of each of the girls, and then posed them at the kitchen island for the group shot.

Afterward, everyone had a soda and talked about school before going home.

"So, are you ready for another quiz in Spontak's class?" Justin asked Molly.

Molly looked down. "I hope so. But I'm definitely having some trouble in that class! How are you doing?"

"Pretty well," said Justin. "You know, there's a tutoring program at school. Seventh- or eighth-graders sign up to be tutors."

"Sounds like a good idea," said Molly. "I'll definitely sign up. 'Cause Amanda's been too busy to help me."

On Friday morning, when the friends got to school, they looked for The Post.

"It's supposed to be stacked here in the main hall," said Natasha. "I guess it's not ready yet. Rats! I was so psyched to see it."

Just then, she saw Ms. Zane. "Hi, Ms. Zane," she called.

"Good morning, Natasha! The paper will be out by lunchtime."

That afternoon, as everyone walked out of the cafeteria, they picked up copies of the paper, which had just been placed on a table during lunch.

"Here it is! Here it is!" said Natasha.

"Look! There we are! Hey, the photo looks great!"

"We're celebrity chefs!"

"Wow, Molly, you got your own picture, too!" There were two photos—the group shot and a large one of Molly at the mixer.

"Cool headline," Shawn told Natasha.

"Thanks! I thought of it," said Natasha proudly, as her eyes quickly scanned the article. She frowned. "It looks really *short*, though...they must have cut a lot."

Everyone was quiet as they began to read the article.

Peichi looked up, having noticed that the hallway had gotten quiet. "*Ohmygosh!* Everyone's gone!"

"Yipes!" cried Molly. Everyone began to trot to class.

Then, over the loudspeaker, they heard a deep voice say: "This is a lockout. Any student not in his or her seat has detention for tardiness and must report to the Main Office."

The girls began to run faster. One by one, they slipped into class before the teacher closed the door.

Molly had the farthest to run. She broke into a sweat when she saw the door to her classroom close. "Oh, no!" she cried. She finally reached the door and grabbed the handle, but it didn't budge.

She'd been locked out!

Breathing hard, Molly stood at the closed door. She looked around. The empty hall was eerily silent.

There was nothing left to do now but head for the Main Office. To get detention, whatever that was. *Like I need this,* she thought.

She walked as slowly as she could up the hall. She passed Amanda's classroom, where right now, Amanda was safe. *Why me?* thought Molly. *I thought the worst part of this day was going to be Miss Spontak's quiz.*

She turned right at the corner. There, up ahead at the end of the corridor, was the Main Office.

Pressing her lips together, Molly went in the door, grim-faced.

Inside, a tiny woman sat behind a desk, practically hidden behind her computer. Her fingers were flying over the keyboard.

Molly cleared her throat. *"Ahem."*

The typing stopped, and the secretary peered around her computer. She wore cat glasses—not the new, hip kind like Shawn wore, but old-fashioned ones with little rhinestone chips in them. Her hair was gray and worn in a tight bun. On her black cardigan, she wore a pin shaped like a cat's head with rhinestone eyes.

"Yes, dear," said the secretary. She had a high-pitched, sweeter voice than Molly'd expected.

At least she called me "dear," thought Molly. *This can't be that bad.*

"Um—hi. I got locked out."

The secretary rolled her eyes. "Those darn lockouts," she said sympathetically. She eyed Molly up and down. "Are you a sixth-grader?"

Molly nodded.

"Just have a seat, dear."

"Have a seat?" asked Molly robotically.

"Yes, dear. I'll be right back. Here, why don't you read this. It's the school newspaper." She handed Molly a copy of <u>The Post</u>, then pulled it back. "Oh, you have one. Well, I'll be right back." She turned and opened a door that said "Principal" on it, and disappeared inside.

Molly's stomach began to hurt. *What's going to happen to me?* she wondered. *First bad grades, and now this! Amanda's getting good grades, plus she's in the play. What's wrong with me?*

She sighed and stared at her picture in <u>The Post</u>. It was a good picture, she decided, even though she hardly ever took a good picture. Amanda was the photogenic one.

It was hard to concentrate as she waited for her punishment, but Molly couldn't help noticing that her name kept popping up all over the article. *That's weird,* she thought. *It's like Natasha decided to focus just on me. Why would she do that?*

Just then, the door creaked open. But it wasn't the principal coming out—just the tiny secretary again, holding a slip of paper.

"There you go, dear," she said.

Molly looked at the piece of paper. It had a signature on it. "Um—what should I do with this?"

"Oh, just go back to class, dear."

"Aren't I, like, supposed to get detention or something?"

"Not this time, dear. You're new here. And I'm sure you didn't intend to be late for class. Did you, dear?"

Molly shook her head.

"So I just told the principal that it was all an accident." The secretary's eyes twinkled behind her cat glasses. "Our little secret, you know. That's your hall pass to get you back to class without any more trouble."

Molly smiled gratefully. "Oh, okay. Well, thank you, Miss—Ms.—"

"Miss Hinkle. Now, off to class with you!" She led Molly to the door.

Molly's classroom door was still locked. She had to knock on the door.

When Mr. Bryant opened the door, he gave her a questioning look. Some kids in the class giggled. Molly handed Mr. Bryant the hall pass.

"Oh, all right," he said. "Have a seat."

Molly sat down. Already, the trip to the principal's office was forgotten. Now she was worrying about something else—why the article was mostly about her...and what the other Chef Girls were going to think about that.

$\mathcal{A}$fter school, Molly decided to try to find Amanda
before she went into rehearsal. She wanted to talk to her
about Natasha's article.

Heading for the drama classroom, she practically ran
into Ms. Barlow. Ms. Barlow was wearing boots with
spiked heels, black pants, and a fuzzy pink sweater. Her
lipstick matched the sweater exactly.

"I'm sorry!" cried Molly.

"Oh, hello, Amanda!" said Ms. Barlow.

"No, I'm Molly, Amanda's twin."

"That's *right!* Amanda has a *twin!* How nice to meet
you, Molly. Why, I just finished reading the article about
you in <u>The Post</u>. You're a star!"

Molly didn't know what to say.

"Ah!" cried Ms. Barlow. "I just had an *amazing* idea!"

"Is it about the dinner theater?" asked Molly. She
smiled and added, "Amanda told me about that. We were
thinking of asking you if we could help with that, but—"
She stopped. It was too embarrassing to tell Ms. Barlow
about her grades and what Mom had said.

"Yes!" said Ms. Barlow. She hadn't even noticed that
Molly had stopped herself. "In the past, we've used a

caterer. Joe Minelli. He sits on the school board. But I'll tell you *what...*" Ms. Barlow looked both ways and then said in a dramatically low voice, "I do *not* care for his desserts. Last year, they were *awful!* I couldn't eat one cookie—they were so hard I thought I'd crack a tooth! And the *cake!* It was like cardboard! If you girls could do the baking—say, some cookies and a cake—you know, a sheet cake, nothing fancy—I'd be *thrilled!* Really *thrilled!* We'll pay you, of course. We can work that out later."

Molly froze. And then...

"Sure," she heard herself saying. "We could do the baking. How many people come to the dinner theater?"

"We get about fifty people each night, and there are three performances. So, you're baking for one hundred fifty people. Okay? Got to run, Mary. Thanks *so* much! Let me know if you have any questions!"

"Uh, it's Molly," said Molly. "Thanks, Ms. Barlow." But Ms. Barlow was already clicking her way down the hall, waving at students and fellow teachers.

Now what have I done? thought Molly. *How could I have just said that Dish would do the job when I can't even help? Oh, well, maybe the others will do it without me.* Molly swallowed hard. The day was beginning to feel completely out of control! *I'd better get home before anything else happens.*

Just then, she saw Amanda with Tessa, who she knew from gym.

"Hi!" said Amanda. "You know Tessa, right?"

"Hi," said Molly and Tessa to each other.

"I need to talk to you, Amanda," said Molly.

"Oh! Well, we're just about to meet with the dialogue coach," said Amanda. "You know, tomorrow's our speed-through."

"Speed-through?" asked Molly.

"You know. That's when the whole cast sits around a table, and we go through our lines really fast," explained Amanda. "It's to make sure everyone knows their lines by heart." She turned to Tessa. "Can you believe they've finished building the sets already? They're so cool!"

"I know!" said Tessa.

"Sets?" asked Molly.

Amanda turned back to Molly. "Yeah! You know, the scenery for the play. Connor and Omar were on the set crew. They helped build the London street scene. It looks so real!" She turned back to Tessa. "I can't wait for tech."

"Neither can I," said Tessa.

"Tech?" asked Molly.

Amanda turned to Molly. "Tech is a special rehearsal. We run the whole show so that the lighting crew knows their cues to change the lights and stuff. And the sound crew knows when to make sound effects."

"Oh," said Molly, still confused. "Well, anyway, do you have time to walk me out?"

"Okay. Tessa, I'll see you in a minute." Amanda headed down the hall with Molly.

"So what's with that article?" asked Amanda.

Molly looked at her anxiously. "I know. Why did Natasha write so much about me? Why is that picture of me so big?"

Amanda shrugged. "I don't know. But I wouldn't worry about it."

"But I *am* worried about it. What are Shawn and Peichi going to think? This article makes it sound like it was my idea to start a business. But it was Shawn's idea!"

"Well," said Amanda with a shrug, "Shawn wasn't even *around* for the interview. And Peichi had to leave. Natasha didn't have time to interview them separately, so don't worry about *them*. But for some reason, I'm not mentioned much, and I was there!" She chuckled. "Oh, well. Maybe she'll mention me in her article about the play!" She laughed again. "She owes me."

Me, me, me, thought Molly. *That's all Amanda thinks about these days.* Molly sighed. "I'm going to call Natasha about it tonight. Well, see you later."

"Okay. Bye."

"I can't believe it," Natasha said on the phone later to Molly. "Lena cut my article to fit the space in the paper.

She says that there was no time to show it to me. But she practically rewrote it!"

"Oh!" said Molly. "That's why it's so wrong!"

"Lena changed the facts!" Natasha went on. "She edited out so much stuff. And she's the one that wanted the big picture of you. I think that's just a coincidence, but...I just wish that she had let me see the article after she cut it. I would have made her change a few things. Now the article's practically all about you!"

"I know," said Molly.

"I just hope that Shawn, Peichi, and Amanda aren't too upset with me," said Natasha. "Ugh. I finally make some new friends, and *this* has to happen!"

"Oh, Natasha, I'm sure everyone will understand when you explain it to them," said Molly. "Don't worry so much."

"I just hope they give me a chance to explain," said Natasha sadly.

Molly showed Mom the article and told her what had happened.

"It sounds like Natasha's had her first experience with bad editing," said Mom. "Don't worry. The other girls will understand."

"Oh, Mom," said Molly. "I had a terrible day. This

article isn't even all of it. I think I flunked another quiz."

Mom did not look happy.

"But Justin told me about student tutoring," Molly went on. "Our school has students who help other students. I think I should sign up for a tutor. Don't you?"

Mom nodded. "Yes, I do," she said. "This is getting serious. I want you to sign up on Monday. Okay?"

"Okay. And—and there's something else I have to tell you."

"What is it?" Mom looked anxious.

"I—I told Ms. Barlow that—that Dish would make the desserts for the dinner theater for *My Fair Lady*."

"Oh," said Mom. She didn't look mad. "Well, that's not so bad. I just don't know that you will be able to help with the job."

"The play's still a while off," Molly pointed out. "If I get my grades up, I can do the job, right?"

"Right. And I know you'll get your grades back up. You'll get a tutor at school, and if that doesn't work, we'll get outside help. Whatever it takes. Okay, sweetheart?"

Both Molly and Natasha really wanted to talk to the other girls. They needed to clear the air about the article, and Molly wanted to bring up the dinner theater job.

But it was harder and harder to get everyone together.

The next day, Peichi met up with Molly and Amanda, and they walked to Harry's.

"It's been such a long time since we were here!" said Peichi. "I've missed this place!"

"*Mmm*, so have I," said Amanda. "I haven't had one of these blondies since forever."

Molly told Peichi about her conversation with Natasha. "...so you see, Natasha wrote the article about all of us, but the editor slanted it differently. You're not mad at Natasha, are you? Or me?"

"No, I'm not mad," said Peichi. "Actually, it's kind of funny! I'll call Natasha and tell her I'm not mad. And I'll tell her how good the article was. It really was! And it was fun seeing my picture. *Our* picture."

The twins smiled at each other. Peichi hardly ever got mad. She was so easy to be around.

"So I have some Dish news," Molly announced. "Amanda knows it already, of course. But I talked with Ms. Barlow, and she would like to hire us to do the desserts for the *My Fair Lady* dinner theater."

"Tell Peichi why, Molly," ordered Amanda with a giggle.

"Oh, yeah! You should've heard her! She was talking about this guy, Joe Minelli? He's on the school board. And he has a restaurant, so he caters the show every year. But she said that his desserts stunk! That she practically broke

115

a tooth on a cookie and that the cake tasted like card-board! Can you believe she said that!"

All the girls cracked up.

"That sounds great!" said Peichi. "And it sounds easy. We can do cookies and sheet cakes no problem."

"That's what I thought," said Molly. "Of course, I have to get my grades up before I can really say I can help. Hey, where's Shawn? Isn't she coming?"

"Oh, she's with Angie What's-Her-Name," said Amanda, waving her hand in the air.

"Is Natasha coming?"

"No, she's watching a closed rehearsal for the two leads of the play. They're working on their big scene. Justin's there, too," said Amanda, "He's like the official photographer or some-thing." She took a mirror out of her bag and put on her lip gloss. "Who wants to read lines with me? I have the script right here."

Peichi and Molly groaned.

"I'm *running* to get another lemonade," announced Amanda, "but I'll be right back. If you could turn to page twenty-two, that'd be a *huge* help. Thank you, *darling!*"

Peichi and Molly giggled.

"She's starting to sound like Ms. Barlow!" whispered Molly, and the girls cracked up again.

chapter 13

Monday came too quickly for Molly. She was nervous about requesting a tutor. But deep down, something told her that things were going to get better soon, just like Mom had said.

Molly put in her request, and the next day after school, she nervously reported to the Main Office once again. This time it was to meet her tutor. What if she didn't like her? What if the tutor was going to treat her like some dummy?

Molly opened the door and Miss Hinkle peered from around her computer. She stood up. "Hello, dear!"

The girl was already there waiting for Molly. She gave Molly a gentle smile. "Hi, are you Molly? I'm Athena Vardalos," she said. She was very tall for a seventh-grader. Her deep brown eyes were the same color as her glossy, wavy hair.

Molly relaxed and smiled. "Hi, Athena."

"Let's head over to the cafeteria," suggested Athena. "No one's in there right now, and it'll be quiet."

As the girls walked down the hall, they chatted easily.

"You look familiar," Athena told Molly.

"Oh," said Molly, blushing, "maybe it's because there's a photo of me in last week's Post."

"That's it! You're the girl who has her own cooking business!"

"Well—it's not just me! I do it with my twin sister and three friends."

"Oh, right."

The girls sat down at a long table in the cafeteria. It was quiet except for a far-off clatter of dishes and the voices of a few remaining kitchen workers.

"Well, what do you want to work on? Let's see your last math quiz." Athena smiled sympathetically. "I had Miss Spontak last year."

"Here," said Molly, handing over the "red" quiz. She knew that Athena wouldn't laugh at it.

The next day, Molly sat in the middle of her friends during lunch.

"I've been thinking about the desserts for the dinner theater," she told them. "You know, it's coming up soon! Instead of doing sheet cakes, we could make cupcakes, and decorate them with cute little drawings from the play, like the big hats, or flowers. Wouldn't that be cute?"

"It sounds like a lot more work than

doing a sheet cake," Peichi pointed out. "We'd have to decorate each cupcake individually."

"But there are five of us," Molly said. "We could do them pretty quickly. It would only be, like, thirty each."

"You know, I think I'm going to be too busy to help with this job, after all," said Peichi. "I'm learning Chinese after school, and I've got the play. Do you mind?"

"Uh, no, that's okay," Molly said disappointedly. "We still have enough people."

"I have a test next period," Shawn groaned, changing the subject. "I can't wait until it's over!"

"Did you start your English paper yet, Amanda?" asked Peichi.

"But of course, *dahling*," said Amanda in her British accent.

There she goes again with that bad British accent! thought Molly. "So, anyway, what do you guys think of my idea?" Molly was starting to get annoyed with her friends. *Doesn't anyone have any ideas about this job besides me?*

"Sounds good," replied Shawn.

"It's cute," added Natasha.

"Sounds good," said Amanda absently. She sighed. "I wonder if I'll have stage fright? What if I forget my lines?"

The next few weeks were pretty normal for all of the girls. Molly was practicing the piano and studying hard. She worked with Athena a few times a week. And it was beginning to pay off! Each of Miss Spontak's quizzes seemed easier, and each one brought fewer red slashes. Mom and Dad were relieved and told Molly how proud they were of her hard work.

"So does this mean I can do the Dish job for *My Fair Lady*?" asked Molly.

Mom and Dad looked at each other. They nodded.

"As long as your grades don't slip back down," warned Mom.

About a week before the play opened, Amanda and Shawn arranged to hang out after school, just the two of them, before cheerleading practice and rehearsal began.

"We could go get a slice of pizza," Amanda had suggested, "and then walk back to school."

"Sounds good," said Shawn. "I'll meet you in front of the school."

But that afternoon, Amanda waited and waited, and Shawn didn't show up.

Amanda thought about going back into the school to look for her, but worried that Shawn wouldn't find her where they were supposed to meet.

Amanda stood, she sat, and she paced. Finally it was time for rehearsal, so she headed back inside, confused.

Did I get the day wrong? she wondered. *Does Shawn think we're doing this tomorrow?*

Amanda made her way to the auditorium. When she walked in the door, she smiled to herself. She couldn't believe she was a part of this—this set, this music, this excitement that was building every day.

Some of the set crew were touching up the paint on the London street set. It had columns and a large, beautiful doorway to represent a church, two street lamps, and a building that looked like a theater. The floor was covered with fake cobblestones. Behind the wooden structure was a painted backdrop of shops.

"Hi, Omar," called Amanda.

Omar nodded and waved.

Amanda was still too early for rehearsal, so she decided to walk by the gym to see if Shawn was there.

As she got closer, Amanda thought she recognized Shawn's voice echoing in the hall. She turned the corner, and there was Shawn, with Angie and a few other girls. They were talking and laughing loudly.

"Oh, hi," said Shawn when she saw Amanda. "What's up?"

The group of girls instantly grew quiet. They all stared at Amanda.

What's up? What's up? fumed Amanda. Was Angie sneering at her? What was that *look* for?

"Oh, hi," said Amanda, trying to mimic Shawn's

casualness. She had to think fast. She wasn't about to say to Shawn, "Where were you?"

"I—I'm just looking for Tessa," Amanda heard herself say. "We have to head to rehearsal now. It's a big one today."

"Tessa's not here," said Angie in her shrill voice. She reached her arm out as long as it could go, and pointed a long fingernail in the direction Amanda had just come from. "Rehearsal's in the auditorium. This is the *gym*."

The girls began to crack up. Their laughter echoed and bounced off the walls, hitting Amanda in her ears, her stomach, her throat. She knew her neck and face were turning red, but there was nothing she could do about it.

She tried to keep a casual look on her face, even as she panicked inside. Then she looked at Shawn—who was looking down at the floor. *At least Shawn's not laughing,* thought Amanda.

She had to get out of there. But there was no way she was going to walk in the direction Angie had just pointed her toward. So she put one shaky foot in front of the other, walked past the girls, and said something like, "See ya later," when she passed Shawn.

"See ya," Shawn had practically whispered.

Amanda didn't look at her this time.

As Amanda walked away, the sound of her own heart pounding in her ears drowned out the sounds of the girls' sharp laughter.

Amanda went through rehearsal in a daze. Her voice seemed brittle when she sang or spoke her lines. Tessa wasn't there because she was sick. Everything felt off.

When Amanda got home from rehearsal, she found Molly, Matthew, and Mom in the kitchen, playing Scrabble.

"Hi," said Amanda from the doorway.

No one heard her because they were laughing.

Matthew spotted her first. "Hi!" he said. "Wanna play? You and me against Mom and Molly?"

Amanda shook her head and turned around. Suddenly, her eyes filled with tears. She could relax now that she was home. She began to cry, and ran upstairs to be alone.

She didn't even hear Mom and Molly come into the room.

"What's the *matter*?" they both asked, sitting down on her bed.

"Shawn completely bl—blew me off." Amanda began to cry again, louder.

"Oh, sweetheart," said Mom. She stroked Amanda's

hair. "You know, Shawn called here earlier. She said she'd call you later."

"I don't want to t—talk to her." Amanda took the tissue that Mom offered her, blew her nose, and sat up. "She's hanging out with the meanest people."

"What happened?" asked Mom.

Amanda told them everything.

Molly looked at Mom. "Yeah, that Angie Martinez. She's really stuck-up. And loud and stuff."

Mom didn't say anything for a moment. "Was Shawn mean to you?" she asked.

"Well, no. It was just the girls she was with."

"When she calls back, just listen to what she has to say. Okay, sweetheart?"

Amanda didn't say anything. She crumpled up her tissue and tossed it toward the wicker wastebasket. She missed.

"People change," said Mom softly, leaning over to pick up the tissue ball. She placed it in the wastebasket. "Sometimes friendships change. You're all changing and growing up, and sometimes it's going to feel like nothing's the same from day to day."

"That's for sure," said the twins at the same time.

"You'll give Shawn another chance, I hope," said Mom as she rubbed Amanda's shoulders. "You've been friends too long to do otherwise."

"I know," said Amanda. She began to sniffle. Then she turned her head away from Mom and Molly.

Mom pointed to the door, Molly nodded, and the two got up. They could tell Amanda wanted to be by herself for a while.

"What about twins?" Molly asked Mom sadly when they got to the kitchen. "Do twins change? Amanda seems far away from me. She's always talking in that British accent. And all she talks about is the play. And Tessa. And the play. And Tessa."

Mom smiled. "Yes, Amanda's pretty self-absorbed right now!" she chuckled. Then her expression turned sincere. "But Amanda loves you as much as she ever did, sweetheart. She's just going through a new experience that means a lot to her. But don't worry. Amanda will always, *always* be there for you. Let's just be patient with her, okay? Pretty soon the play will be over, and she'll be back to normal. I promise!"

Molly nodded. She hoped Mom was right. Then Molly noticed that the message light on the answering machine was blinking.

"That's funny," said Mom. "I didn't hear the phone ring."

"Amanda was crying too loud," chuckled Molly. She pushed the button.

Beep!

"Hello," said a voice. "This is Natasha. Um, Molly and

125

Amanda, I, um, can't help with the dessert job for *My Fair Lady*. I'm sorry. My mom says I'm in over my head. With homework and Hebrew school and the article about the play. Okay? I'm sorry. Uh, see-you-tomorrow-bye."

Briiinnnnggg! The phone rang just as the message finished playing.

"Hello?" said Molly.

"Hi, Molls, it's Shawn."

"Oh. Hi, Shawn."

There was a pause. "Um, is Amanda there?"

"Hang on a minute. She's upstairs. I'll get her."

Molly put down the phone, then ran up the stairs, two at a time. She opened the bedroom door. Amanda looked up from her science textbook.

"Shawn?" asked Amanda.

Molly nodded.

Usually Molly and Amanda talked to Shawn together, but this time, when Molly heard Amanda get on the upstairs extension, Molly hung up.

After a while, Molly went upstairs. Amanda was doing her homework at the desk.

"So?" asked Molly.

"She was really sorry. She said she totally forgot we

were supposed to meet. She feels really bad about the way Angie and her friends acted."

"So, are you okay?" asked Molly.

"I'm fine." Amanda sighed heavily. "But you know what bums me out the most? That Shawn forgot we were getting together today. *I'd* never forget."

"I know," said Molly. She didn't know what to say about that. It did seem strange that Shawn had forgotten.

"By the way," said Amanda, "Shawn also said that she can't help with the dessert job. She's just gotten way too busy."

"Oh, *great*. Now it's just the *two* of us," said Molly. "How are we going to do all that baking?"

Amanda sighed. She looked down at her book.

That's when Molly knew that Amanda didn't want to work on the job, either. Or couldn't work on it. *Whatever. Too bad—she's going to have to do it anyway. What's happening with Dish? Doesn't anyone care except me? Mom's right—nothing seems the same anymore!* Molly thought.

The next day, Molly met Athena at their usual table in the empty cafeteria.

"Hi, Molly!" said Athena. She sat down and said, "How are you?"

"I'm okay, I guess," replied Molly, trying to be cheerful. "How are you?"

"You don't seem okay," observed Athena. "Did something happen in math class?"

"No," she said. "I'm just a little worried because Dish is supposed to make the desserts for the *My Fair Lady* dinner theater. But there's no Dish right now, except for my sister and me!"

"Oh, no!" said Athena. Her brown eyes opened wide. "That's terrible! What do you have to make?"

"Oh, cookies. And some cake. I had wanted to make cupcakes and decorate them for the play. You know, put little drawings on with icing—"

"Oh, that's a good idea," said Athena. "I've seen *My Fair Lady*. You could draw little hats, and gloves, and flowers—"

Molly gasped. "That's exactly what I wanted to do!" she exclaimed.

Athena grinned. "Great minds think alike," she said. "Well, I'll help you! If you want me to."

"Really?" cried Molly. "That would be great! Thank you so much!"

Athena smiled again. "I have some free time. Just tell me what to do. You'll be the boss. Okay? Now, let's take a look at your math homework."

At play rehearsal the next day, everyone was a little edgy, especially Bruce MacMillan, the eighth-grader who was playing Henry Higgins, and Tiffany Hurst, who was playing Eliza Doolittle. They'd been arguing with each other.

"We're doing a full run next Monday and Tuesday," Ms. Barlow reminded everyone. "That means we're doing the whole play! In order! With the orchestra! The lights! We open on Thursday night. There is a six thirty call starting Monday night. Don't be late, people— or you'll give me a heart attack wondering where you are!"

"What's 'call'?" asked someone.

"That means you are expected here at six thirty to give you time for makeup, costumes, and warm-up," explained Ms. Barlow.

Amanda looked over at Natasha, who was watching

this rehearsal. She was busily writing down everything Ms. Barlow was saying. Justin was near her, loading his camera. *Those two are always together,* thought Amanda. *She and Justin are better friends than I'll ever be with him.*

"I can't wait for next week!" chattered Tessa as she and Amanda waited backstage with the others for their cues. "It's going to be so cool! We'll eat popcorn and

 put makeup on each other, and take pictures of everyone, and do a group warm-up, and hang out until it's time to go onstage."

"I hadn't even thought about all that," said Amanda.

"Oh, Tiffany was telling me that being in the green-room with everyone before the play is the best part! Everyone's really excited, and joking, and laughing together."

"What's the greenroom?" Amanda wanted to know.

"You know, where the actors hang out before it's their turn to go onstage. And everyone goes back there when they come offstage."

"Sounds like fun," stated Amanda. "It must feel like you're in a real theater troupe."

"Ex-*actly!*"

Amanda walked home that night with Natasha.

"I didn't do so well tonight," Amanda complained.

"Really? I thought you were great."

"No, I stumbled over my lines and my accent came out all wrong. Could you hear me okay?"

"Sure. Don't worry so much," Natasha told her.

Amanda couldn't get rid of the nervous feeling in her stomach. How was she going to help Molly with all the baking? Both of them had a lot of studying over the weekend for exams. And next week was already full.

That night after dinner, she tried to start her math homework, but she couldn't concentrate.

"Molls," she blurted. Molly was sitting at the desk, while she was on the floor, her back against her bed. "I don't see how I can help you and Athena with the baking."

Molly looked up from her book. She couldn't believe what she was hearing!

"I can't do it. I just can't. I've got tests next week—and the play! We have dress rehearsals every night!"

Molly slammed her heavy science book closed. Her eyes showed panic. "You *have* to help! We need you!" She was starting to really freak out.

"Well," said Amanda, as she searched for something to say. "Can't you just tell Ms. Barlow it's—it's not going to work out?"

"Tell her *what?*" shrieked Molly. "It's too late to back out now! How would she find someone else? *You* tell her!"

Amanda didn't say anything.

"Thanks for nothing," snapped Molly. "You've been acting like such a big shot ever since you got in this play. You've been driving everyone crazy. Peichi—"

"What about Peichi?"

"She told me that you wanted her to change your costume."

Amanda rolled her eyes. "That was no big deal."

"How do you think it made Peichi feel? She got over it—she always does—but, come on! And then Natasha—you practically ordered her to mention in her article about Dish that you were in the play."

Amanda blushed. She didn't say anything.

"And me! You're always walking around with your hand on your hip, speaking in that accent! You think you're so cool. All you talk about is the play. You barely listen to anything I have to say anymore."

Amanda's mouth dropped open. She couldn't believe the things Molly was saying. They were *so* not true! And yet...was there a tiny chance that she *had* been that obnoxious?

Amanda tried to speak, but nothing came out.

"Okay," she finally said. "I'll help with the baking. We can start this weekend—"

"Never mind," said Molly. "I don't want you to help anymore. I really don't."

"That's ridiculous, Molls," said Amanda. "I'm sorry."

But Molly ignored Amanda the rest of the evening, despite Amanda's dramatic sighs. And the next morning, Molly left for school before Amanda was ready.

Molly and Mom had a talk the next day.

"You said Amanda would always be there for me," Molly reminded Mom. "But she's not."

"Don't give up on her just yet," said Mom, which made Molly roll her eyes. "And don't worry about the desserts," Mom went on. "You and I are going to start right now. And I'm sure Athena will be a big help."

Molly sighed. "I know you're busy, too, Mom. This is your busiest time working at the college."

Mom put her arms around Molly. "What do you want to bake?" she asked. "I can't wait to do all this. I've really missed cooking with you—like we did all summer!"

At rehearsal that afternoon, Ms. Barlow gave the cast a pep talk.

"This is it, people. We open in three days. You're all doing great, and now I want to see you all being more confident, more in character. Give it your *all!* People are spending good money to come see you perform! Show 'em what you've *got!*"

The cast cheered.

"Oh! I have another announcement," said Ms. Barlow. "There will be a cast party at my house on Saturday night after the play. Everyone who has worked on the play is invited."

The cast cheered again.

"This week," said Ms. Barlow, "you have *such* an important job to do. Acting is all about giving. Giving everything you have…"

But Amanda knew she had something even more important to do. Something she had to *give up.*

Right after rehearsal, she stood in front of Ms. Barlow until Ms. Barlow could give her some attention.

"What is it, Amanda?" asked Ms. Barlow. She suddenly looked away, distracted. "Morgan! I almost forgot. Please trade hats with Amber. Hers matches your dress better—Tiffany, let's talk in the morning before homeroom."

"Ms. Barlow, I need to ask you something," began Amanda. "It's—kind of important."

 134

"So, you see, I can help with the baking," Amanda told Molly that night. She and Molly were helping Mom clear the dinner dishes.

Mom smiled at Molly, as if to say, *I told you so!*

"But how can you do that?" asked Molly. She still didn't believe Amanda. "You have to get ready for the play. You have to be there early, even on Wednesday."

"Ms. Barlow said that as long as I'm in costume and makeup and in the greenroom by seven forty-five sharp on opening night, it'll be fine," Amanda began to explain. "It's a big deal that she's letting me come late, because she doesn't want to worry. So, anyway, we'll have time to bake and decorate the cupcakes. And you, Mom, and Athena made the chocolate-chip cookies already. So a lot's already been done."

"Yeah, they turned out great," said Molly. She was trying to say something nice to Amanda, but that's all she could come up with. She was still a little upset.

"Molly, Amanda's giving up something important," said Mom gently. "Opening night is a big deal for the cast and crew..."

"Everyone's going to be, you know, having a great time backstage, putting on makeup, and taking pictures of each other," Amanda tried to explain to Molly. *Uh-oh,* she thought. She was going to start crying. She looked up at the kitchen light to try to keep the tears from falling.

"And you're going to miss all that?" Molly asked. She was beginning to "get" what Amanda was talking about. "Being with your friends before you go onstage."

"Uh-huh."

"Well, thanks. That's—that's really nice of you."

That night, while Amanda was in the shower, Molly hurried down to the den and began to type.

To: happyface; qtpie490; BrooklynNatasha
From: mooretimes2
Re: Amanda's big night!

I know we're all going to see Amanda in the play together on Friday night, but . . . just a reminder that opening night is Thursday! So call here late that afternoon to tell Amanda to "Break a leg!" (Amanda sez that's theater talk for "Good luck.")

It's so exciting. Mom and Dad and Matthew and I are giving her a bouquet

of flowers Friday night. *Sshh!* It's a
surprise!

    Mwa! Molly

Thursday afternoon came quickly.

The kitchen smelled of chocolate cupcakes. They were
on their fourth double batch, thanks to Mom, who'd
decided to take the day off to jump-start the baking.
They'd baked them and iced them and now they were
beginning to decorate them. The chocolate-chip cookies
were all done and were packed in tins, ready to be
delivered.

"These cupcakes don't smell as chocolatey as
yesterday," complained Matthew.

"That's just because you've been smelling them for
two days now," said Mom crisply. "Listen, girls. We may
not have time to decorate all of these cupcakes. But at
least they'll all be iced."

"But we *have* to decorate them," muttered Molly.

Athena looked at her watch. "I hate to bail now, but
I really have to get home. *I* have a math test I have to
study for."

Molly smiled. "That's okay. You've been a great help.
Besides, how would it look if my tutor flunked a test?"

Athena laughed and headed out the door.

"I have to take a break to help Amanda with her makeup," said Mom. "You and Matthew keep working."

Twenty minutes later, Amanda was in costume, except for her hat and shawl—she would put those on at the last minute. Mom had helped her make up her face to look like it had soot on it. Her hair was pulled up in an old-fashioned-style bun.

"There," said Mom, as the two looked at Amanda's reflection in the big mirror. "You look great!"

That's when Amanda realized something.

Her costume wasn't too dark or too uncool. It was perfect for the role of flower seller number four. Her role was a small one, but it was just as important as anyone else's. And it was important that she look—just like this.

Amanda went downstairs and got right back to work.

She put the finishing touch on the cupcake she was decorating, then held it up. "See? Does that look like a high-button shoe?"

"That's cute, Manda," said Molly.

"Hold that pose!" cried Mom. "I'll take a picture. Say Flower Seller!"

Amanda smiled, posed with the cupcake, and said, "Flower Seller!"

Just then, the doorbell rang.

"I'll get it!" cried Matthew.

Footsteps and giggles came down the hallway to the kitchen. It was Peichi, Shawn, and Natasha—wearing their chef's aprons!

"BREAK A LEG, AMANDA!" they all cried, as Molly and Mom looked on in surprise.

Shawn handed Amanda a bouquet of colorful flowers. "They're from the three of us," she said.

Natasha gave her a big card, decorated with Shawn's cool designs drawn with a glitter pen. And Peichi gave her a big, bright red fabric flower. "For your hat," she said. "We'll pin it on."

"*Ohmygosh!*" shrieked Amanda.

She hugged her friends and said, "No one's ever given me flowers before! And I love the pin! Thank you!"

"You look great!" exclaimed Shawn. "I love your costume!"

"Thank you very much!" said Peichi, and everyone laughed.

"I love my costume, too," said Amanda, looking at Peichi. "Thanks, Peichi." She gave her a hug.

"Oh, Amanda, you look so cute with your dirty face," chuckled Natasha.

Just then, the friends looked around.

"Well, let's get to work!" said Shawn. "We have to wash our hands. Move out of the way, Amanda. An actress can't get her costume dirty before the show!"

"Get together!" said Mom, picking up her camera.

"Wait! Let me put on the rest of my costume," said Amanda.

Mom snapped the photo when Amanda was ready. "That was a good one!" she cried. "Come on, one more. Say 'Amanda!'"

"Amanda!" cried the girls.

After the photo was taken, Shawn whispered into Amanda's ear. "While you were in line for your food at lunch today, I told everyone to meet at my house after school to sign the card. And the three of us talked, and everyone said they wanted to be here today to help out! I'm so sorry about...everything. I've missed you."

"Me, too," whispered Amanda.

Amanda had one more thing to do.

"Excuse me! Time out!" she called over all the chatter. "Sorry if I've driven some of you a little nuts lately," she said. "You guys are the best friends in the world."

Moments later, Molly looked around at the kitchen. Her friends filled it up with their talk and laughter. Sugar crunched underneath her shoes. Shawn already had flour in her hair. Everything felt—normal!

"It's nice to be the Chef Girls again," she said.

chapter 176

Soon it was time for Amanda to go. She picked up her shawl and hat, now with the red flower pinned to it.

"Good-bye! Break a leg!" cried everyone, even Matthew.

Molly gave Amanda a quick hug. "You'll be great," said Molly. "Congratulations."

"Bye, everybody!" called Amanda.

After Mom walked Amanda into the school, she said, "Okay, honey." She hugged her carefully so that she wouldn't smudge Amanda's makeup. "Break a leg! Dad and I will be in the audience tonight. We'll find you after the show."

"Thanks, Mom! Thanks for everything today!"

Amanda could hear the buzz of everyone in the greenroom. Her heart began to pound.

This was it!

As she walked into the greenroom, Tessa ran over to her with a little shriek. "Hi! Hi! Hi! You're here! *Ohmygosh!*"

"Yeah, I made it!" said Amanda. "You look great! Nice and sooty!"

"So do you!"

The two girls giggled and walked around the green-room, checking everyone out. Some, like Tiffany, were calm, sitting quietly by themselves. Some were saying their lines over and over. Some stretched and did breathing exercises.

Everyone was in full makeup and costume, just like last night's dress rehearsal. But tonight felt so different from last night.

"This ain't no rehearsal," one of the boys kept saying in a funny voice.

Ms. Barlow appeared, smiling and calm. She looked stunning in her short, red velvet cocktail dress and glittering diamond earrings.

"Let's make a circle," she said. Everyone quickly grabbed hands and formed a large ring.

They all became silent.

"You're wonderful, all of you," said Ms. Barlow. "The most talented, enthusiastic group of kids I've ever worked with. Thank you."

More silence.

"Now," she continued, "Have a *fabulous* opening night! It's time to give it your all! Break a leg, everybody!"

"Wooooo-*oooh!*" Everyone whooped and threw up their arms.

Suddenly, Sam Wong appeared in his headset. He was

the stage manager and was responsible for making the show run smoothly.

"Places," he announced.

A gasp went up all over the room. It was time for the show to begin!

"That's us!" said Tessa. She and Amanda were both in act one, though they were just extras for the street scene.

Grabbing each other's hands, Amanda and Tessa followed the rest of the act one group down the hall, through a door, and onto the stage. They quietly took their places where they'd been assigned to stand.

The curtain was still down, of course. Behind the curtain, the actors could hear the buzz of the audience as they found their seats and talked and rustled their programs. *The audience is excited, too,* Amanda realized.

The orchestra was finishing warming up. A piccolo trilled and a cymbal went *chinnngg.*

Amanda looked around the stage. The London street set looked so beautiful with the stage lighting. *It's real, but not real, at the same time,* thought Amanda. *Like a street in a dream.*

As she gazed at the other kids, quiet and thinking their own thoughts, Amanda felt like she was in a dream, too.

Suddenly, all was quiet.

Then, *BOOM!* A drum rumbled, and the overture began. As the music played, Amanda felt like an electrical current had run right through her. The curtain began to rise, and the actors began to move as people would on a busy street at night.

Amanda looked out into the sea of blurry faces. She felt the warmth of a spotlight as it hit her face. And she began to laugh and joke as part of the crowd that watches Eliza Doolittle and Henry Higgins argue back and forth.

She'd done it. She'd taken a chance. Gone to the audition when she could have stayed home. And now she was here, onstage, where she had always belonged.

The Amazing cookbook

By
The CHEF Girls

AMANDA!

Molly!

Peichi ☺

shawn!

Natasha!

GRANDMA RUTHIE'S RED VELVET CAKE

THIS CAKE IS GOOD! IT TASTES BETTER THE DAY AFTER YOU MAKE IT, IF IT LASTS THAT LONG! BECAUSE OF ITS RED COLOR, IT'S NICE FOR A VALENTINE'S DAY PARTY OR FOR CHRISTMAS.

YOU WILL NEED:

A MIXER AND TWO GREASED AND FLOURED 9" ROUND CAKE PANS

1/2 CUP SHORTENING

1 1/2 CUPS SUGAR

2 EGGS

1 TEASPOON VANILLA EXTRACT

3 LEVEL TABLESPOONS COCOA

2 1/2 CUPS SIFTED CAKE FLOUR

1 CUP BUTTERMILK

1 TEASPOON SALT

1 TABLESPOON VINEGAR

1 TEASPOON BAKING SODA

1 TEASPOON BUTTER FLAVORING (IF YOU DON'T HAVE BUTTER FLAVORING, YOU CAN USE AN EXTRA TEASPOON OF VANILLA EXTRACT)

1 1/2 - OUNCE BOTTLE OF RED FOOD COLORING

1. PREHEAT THE OVEN TO 350 DEGREES.

2. CREAM TOGETHER THE SHORTENING, SUGAR, EGGS, VANILLA, AND BUTTER FLAVORING. ("CREAM" MEANS TO WORK OR BLEND THE INGREDIENTS IN THE MIXER UNTIL CREAMY.)

3. NOW MAKE A PASTE OF THE COCOA AND FOOD COLORING BY MIXING THEM TOGETHER. ADD IT TO THE BATTER.

4. ADD THE SALT AND FLOUR ALTERNATELY WITH THE
   BUTTERMILK INTO THE BATTER. (THIS IS SO THAT YOU
   DON'T HAVE TO WORK WITH A BIG LUMP OF FLOUR.)
5. MIX BAKING SODA AND VINEGAR IN A SMALL BOWL;
   ADD IT TO THE BATTER.
6. BLEND. POUR THE BATTER INTO THE TWO GREASED
   AND FLOURED CAKE PANS.
7. BAKE FOR 25-30 MINUTES.
   LET THE CAKE COOL COMPLETELY,
   THEN COVER WITH THE FROSTING.

FROSTING
2 PACKAGES CREAM CHEESE (3 OUNCES EACH), SOFTENED
6 TABLESPOONS BUTTER, SOFTENED
1 TEASPOON VANILLA EXTRACT
2 CUPS SIFTED POWERED SUGAR

   BLEND ALL INGREDIENTS UNTIL SMOOTH.

Mr. Moore's
Oatmeal Pancakes

I don't cook much, but I do make great pancakes on Saturday mornings! These are really good with 1 cup blueberries, too! Ask an adult to help you ladle the batter onto the hot griddle.

1½ cups rolled oats
2 cups buttermilk
1 teaspoon sugar
½ cup flour
1 teaspoon baking soda
1 teaspoon salt
2 eggs, beaten with fork

You'll need to use a mixer to make the batter. Mix together the oats and buttermilk. Beat in the rest of the ingredients. If you are using blueberries, stir them in last by hand after you have made the batter.

Then ladle the batter onto the hot griddle. You'll know the pancakes are ready to be turned when you see the bubbles in the batter popping. Yum!

Grandma Ruthie's Corn Bread

Corn bread is easy to make. It tastes great with soup and beans— all kinds of food! I make corn bread all the time. You don't even need a mixer... I just use my eggbeater to beat everything together.

2 eggs
2 cups buttermilk
1 teaspoon baking soda
2 cups cornmeal
1 teaspoon salt

Preheat oven to 400 degrees.
Beat eggs. Then beat in the buttermilk, baking soda, cornmeal, and salt. Pour the batter into the buttered pan. Bake 20–25 minutes or just until "set." Serve hot with butter.

We like honey on ours, too!
Grandma Ruthie

P.S. You can also make corn sticks or muffins if you have the right pans. Bake these for 10–15 minutes or just until "set." The pans for corn sticks usually have tins that are shaped like corncobs. A regular muffin pan will do for the muffins.

Grandma Ruthie's Barbecued Brisket

we always have this on the fourth of July and for family reunions. And I always asks for it on my birthday! this recipe should serve 8-10 people.

- one whole brisket
- one bottle of barbecue sauce
- 1/4 cup liquid smoke
- 1/4 cup Worcestershire sauce
- celery salt, garlic salt, onion salt
- salt and pepper to taste
- 10-12 hamburger buns

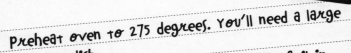

Preheat oven to 275 degrees. You'll need a large glass baking dish.

Place a very large piece of heavy-duty foil in the baking dish. then add the meat, barbecue sauce, liquid smoke, and Worcestershire sauce. then sprinkle the celery, garlic, and onion salts on top, making sure the meat is well-seasoned. wrap the foil tightly around the meat. If possible, marinate the meat this way overnight in the foil. ("marinate" means to let

the meat sit in the liquid so that the flavor sets in.)
Bake five hours in the foil, then uncover and
bake one more hour. Cool about 30 minutes
before slicing (actually, I shred the meat apart).
Serve on large buns. I'll bet everyone has
more than one helping of this!

NOTE: You can bake this meat just 5
hours and skip the 1 additional hour.
That's what Grandma Ruthie usually
does. And you can substitute eye of
the round or sirloin roast for less fat. Enjoy it!

cooking tips
from the chef Girls!

The Chef Girls are looking out for you!
Here are some things you should
know if you want to cook.
(Remember to ask your parents
if you can use knives and the stove!)

1   Tie back long hair so that it won't
    get into the food or in the way as
    you work.

2   Don't wear loose-fitting clothing
    that could drag in the food or
    on the stove burners.

3   Never cook in bare feet or open-toed
    shoes. Something sharp or hot could
    drop on your feet.

4   Always wash your hands before you
    handle food.

5   Read through the recipe before you start. Gather your ingredients together and measure them before you begin.

6   Turn pot handles in so that they won't get knocked off the stove.

7   Use wooden spoons to stir hot liquids. Metal spoons can become very hot.

8   When cutting or peeling food, cut away from your hands.

9   Cut food on a cutting board, not the countertop.

 10   Hand someone a knife with the knifepoint pointing to the floor.

11   Clean up as you go. It's safer and neater.

12   Always use a dry pot holder to remove something hot from the oven. You could get burned with a wet one, since wet ones retain heat.

13   Make sure that any spills on the floor are cleaned up right away, so that you don't slip and fall.

14 Don't put knives in clean-up water. You could reach into the water and cut yourself.

15 Use a wire rack to cool hot baking dishes to avoid scorch marks on the countertop.

An Important Message from the Chef Girls!

Some foods can carry bacteria, such as salmonella, that can make you sick.
To avoid salmonella, always cook poultry, ground beef, and eggs thoroughly before eating.
Don't eat or drink foods containing raw eggs.
And wash hands, kitchen work surfaces, and utensils with soap and water immediately after they have been in contact with raw meat or poultry.

mooretimes2: Molly and Amanda

qtpie490: Shawn

happyface: Peichi

BrooklynNatasha: Natasha

JustMac: Justin

Wuzzup: What's up?

Mwa smooching sound

G2G: Got To Go

deets: details

b-b: Bye-Bye

<3 hearts

L8R: Later, as in "See ya later!"

LOL: Laughing Out Loud

GMTA: Great Minds Think Alike

j/k: Just kidding

B/C: because

W8: Wait

W8 4 me @: Wait for me at

thanx: thanks

BK: Big kiss

MAY: Mad about you

RUF2T?: Are you free to talk?

TTUL: Type to you later

E-ya: will e-mail you

LMK: Let me know

GR8: Great

WFM: Works for me

2: to, too, two

C: see

u: you

2morrow: tomorrow

VH: virtual hug

BFFL: Best Friends For Life

:-@   shock

:-P   sticking out tongue

%-)   confused

:-o   surprised

;-)   winking or teasing